RIVALS

A DRIVEN WORLD NOVEL

Stephanie Nichole

Table of Contents

Copyright Page

This is a work of fiction. Names, characters, organizations, places, events, and incidents are either products of the author's imagination or are used fictitiously. Any resemblance to actual events, locales, or persons living or dead are entirely coincidental.

Ebook Published by JKB Publishing, LLC.
Print Published by Kingston Publishing Company

Cover Design and Formatting by: KP Designs
- www.kpdesignshop.com

Published in the United States of America

Introduction

Dear Reader,

Welcome to the Driven World!

I'm so excited you've picked up this book! Rivals is a book based on the world I created in my *New York Times* bestselling Driven Series. While I may be finished writing this series (*for now*), various authors have signed on to keep them going. They will be bringing you all-new stories in the world you know while allowing you to revisit the characters you love.

This book is entirely the work of the author who wrote it. While I allowed them to use the world I created and may have assisted in some of the plotting, I took no part in the writing or editing of the story. All praise can be directed their way.

I truly hope you enjoy Rivals. If you're interested in finding more authors who have written in the KB Worlds, you can visit www.kbworlds.com.

Thank you for supporting the writers in this project and me.

Happy Reading,
K. Bromberg

Dedication

This book is for everyone, who like me, fell in love with the Driven World. We cheered, cried and fell in love with Colton and Rylee. To see the world continue to grow is beyond exciting and I hope you love it as much as I do.

Prologue

Rathe

I pace back and forth in my trailer, pop another Sour Patch Kids gummy into my mouth and continue my pacing. My fire suit is tied around my waist as I wait for the time to head to the pit. My stomach churns with adrenaline and excitement. It's so strong I can almost reach out, feel it, grab and hold on to it. I run my hands through my hair as I grab another Sour Patch Kid gummy with my free hand. This is my day. This is my race. I've worked so hard for this moment. To win the Grand Prix in my rookie year would be the perfect way to end the race season. I'm good enough to do it. I'm better than every other racer on that track. Maybe, that's cocky of me to think but I know it's true. I was born to do this.

There's a knock on my door and I don't have to open it to know it's my best friend Maxton and probably my twin sister, Ryann. The other two-thirds of the three musketeers. We've been inseparable our entire lives and it'll always be like that. No matter what I can rely on those two through thick and thin. The door opens and Maxton pops his head in. "Time to go," he announces. I see Ryann bouncing on the balls of her feet behind him.

I grab a couple more *Sour Patch Kids* gummies and toss them into my mouth before I grab my Revv-It Racing Team ball cap and a pair of sunglasses. I head down the steps and feel the energy grow tenfold. These are the moments that are so addicting to me. I crave this energy. It's that natural high that nothing else will ever come close to. I see the nerves settle in Ryann's eyes and I wrap an arm around her shoulder. "Don't get that look or I'll have to move you to sit with mom and dad in the stands," I tease her.

She elbows me in the ribs. "That's not funny. I just worry about you."

Maxton steps up on the other side of Ryann and wraps his arm around her shoulders as well. "Ryann don't worry about Rathe. He's got this."

"Damn right," I tell him as I lift my hand for us to bump fists.

Ryann shakes her head and steps away from us. "I'll never understand the male gender."

"That goes both ways, babe," Maxton tells her.

She scoffs. "You know I hate that damn pet name. It's annoying as hell."

"I'm well aware." He starts to laugh and jumps away as she slaps him.

I start to walk away while listening to them bicker. "You two have fun. I have a race to go win."

"Good luck man!" Maxton calls out to me.

I turn around and give them my signature smirk. "This doesn't have anything to do with luck. It's all about the skill and blood, brother," I tell them as I wink before continuing to the pit.

The turquoise of Revv-It Racing is easy to spot. It's a bright spot in the sea of red, blue, black and yellow. Those seem to be what I call the safe colors. Tucker, my crew chief comes up to me and extends my helmet out to me. "Are you ready for this?"

I take the helmet and pat him on the shoulder. "I've been dreaming of this day for years." I take off my ball cap and sunglasses and hand them over. I listen as Tucker gives me all the advice he can about this track. Being a rookie in the Indy race world means I've never driven on any of these tracks before so I listen as he gives me the rundown of his experience. He's got years on these tracks and he's been like a second father to me throughout this year. As good as I am behind the wheel I know that I couldn't have won all of the races I did without him. "Thanks Tucker. It's going to be a hell of a race."

"I'm sure it will be. It's been an honor to have been your crew chief this season," he tells me.

"The honor has been all mine." I pull my fire suit into place and place my helmet on my head. Tucker double checks everything to make sure it's secure then we head to the car. I slide into the car and get comfortable. Tucker gives me a few last words of wisdom and then I'm out of the pit and to the starting line. If someone had told me that at twenty-four I'd be driving in the Indy race world and just had an almost undefeated rookie year I would have laughed at them but I guess sometimes things work out. The stars align or fate steps in...whatever it is you believe in that causes every little piece to fall in place.

The sun beats down and the crowd is energetic. I can feel the blood in my veins pounding with eagerness. I'm ready for this. I take my spot and wait. When the flag drops we all take off and it's like I'm flying, or at least I think this must be what it feels like to fly. The first few laps are steady. As I inch closer and closer to the top spot, car after car I maunevar and pass. Tucker guides me in my blind spots but it's all coming together. I can visualize the win. It's so close I can almost taste it but first I need a pit stop.

Four cars ahead of me, the leader of the pack right now, my Revv-It Racing teammate Chris Ziglar drifts too close to the wall and it's as if I'm watching a movie play out in front of me in slow motion. His car scrapes along the wall and then time speeds up. He spins out of control, smoke fills the air, visibility is gone. Tucker hollers in my ear that he can't see a thing. My heart jumps into my throat and I send up a prayer to something I never believed in before. I'm blind. I have no clue what I'm driving into but there's no time to stop.

More cars join in on the crash and by the time I reach the middle of the smoke filled haze I start to relax. I've made it through the worst of it or so I think. Just as my grip on the steering wheel loosens, I see a flash of red coming towards my driver's side. There's no time to react before it slams into me, knocking me into the wall. I spin out of control and make the rookie mistake of trying to control the spin. Another car slams into me from behind and the next thing I know I'm rolling. Everything flashes before my eyes just before it all goes dark.

One

Sutton

Crossing the finish line puts the biggest smile on my face. I wasn't sure if I had this race won but thankfully I pulled it out. That's another fifteen hundred dollars in my pocket to go towards the rent and utilities. Now the money that Evanna, my best friend and roommate, and I make can go towards food and college classes. I climb out of the car and head over toward Ty, the guy in charge of organizing these street races. We all exchange our congratulations to one another and then the money is dispersed. When I turn around to find Evanna, I spot her easily enough. Her dress sparkles like a disco ball under the street light. However, the sight causes my blood to run cold. I see a man in a fancy suit handing her a card. Men dressed like that don't just show up at the local street races unless they're undercover or something like that.

I pull my hair from the ponytail I had it in and make my way towards her. I'm stopped multiple times and not wanting to be rude I make small chit chat but with every pause I become sicker to my stomach. By the time I make it over to Evanna the guy is gone. "Who was that?" I ask. My voice sounds more demanding than I anticipated.

She shrugs. "Some Indy race scout or something like that. He was interested in you. He said he hadn't seen driving like that in a long time and was highly impressed. He gave me his card and told me to tell you to call him." She extends the card out to me which looks legit but I didn't grow up wearing rose colored glasses. I know that just because something looks legit doesn't mean that it is. Usually, when something seems too good to be

17

true, it is. I shove the business card into the back pocket of my jeans. "You're not going to call him?"

I shake my head. "No, what's the point?"

"The point is that he seemed to be really impressed with your driving Sutton." Evanna crosses her arms and looks at me as if I'm crazy. She is the more trusting of the two of us but it also means she sees the good in everything and sometimes there is no good there, it's just a pretty mask or a nicely put together lie.

"The point is that big time Indy racing scouts are not going to waste their time coming to local street races looking for their next big driver. I don't know how an Indy circuit works exactly but I'm sure there's a more formal way of finding drivers. I'm sure he's just some perv who saw a beautiful girl in a sparkly dress and wanted a reason to talk to her," I explain, giving her a pointed look.

She sighs and rolls her eyes. "He wasn't like that. He only asked about you."

I shrug. "Okay, then he thought my ass looked great in these jeans. Either way he's gone and I'm starving. Can we please go get some pizza now?"

"You're impossible Sutton." Evanna begins to walk towards the car. Once we're heading towards the local pizza place we like to frequent Evanna asks, "How'd you do tonight?"

I smile. "I made more than enough to cover rent and utilities and maybe even a little extra."

Evanna smiles. "That's great!" I drive along with the traffic and the night air blows through the car. I smile as Lenny Kravitz comes on the radio. Evanna looks over at me and we instantly start singing along. Lenny was our favorite singer for years.

Evanna and I grew up together in a roundabout way. I was seven when my father was pulled out of my life. I was shoved into the foster care system. It was a rough three years until I was finally placed in a more stable home. That family managed to keep me until I was sixteen but luckily, Evanna lived next door with her single mother who worked three jobs to make ends meet. Evanna was caring and kind. She would just sit next to me for hours, reading some book because she knew I needed the silence. She grew to become a constant in my life. Having my father yanked away from me had shook my entire world. Throughout the years we've always had each other's backs and always will. She's my sister through and through.

I grab the first parking spot and we climb out of the car. "Are you really not going to call that man?"

"Oh my gosh Evanna! I love you but trust me when I say this, he isn't legit!" I tell her as we stop in the middle of the parking lot.

She throws her hands up in the air like she's frustrated with me. "You don't know that. You didn't even talk to him!"

"I didn't have to. You just have to think about it logically and not with your optimistic mind," I tell her.

Evanna crosses her arms and glares at me. "Says the pessimist. I'll drop it but I think you're making a huge mistake by not at least calling and hearing him out."

I smile at her even though we both know it's fake. "Noted, now can we get the damn pizza?"

"Yes, let's go get your pizza." We order and take a seat. Evanna pushes her very un-appetizing looking salad around before she finally asks, "So, are we going to Jakob's tonight?"

I sigh. Jakob Lane is...was my on again, off again boyfriend until I caught him making out with another girl. Needless, to say I left him quicker than he could offer an apology or some lame ass excuse out. However, Jakob is part of our group of friends and he always throws the best parties after the races. Actually, they aren't so much parties as get-togethers. They're pretty tame in comparison to some of the other stuff going on. The problem is I haven't talked to Jakob in weeks. I haven't been to one of his parties and I avoid him at the races. I'm not sure if I want to change that now. "I don't know. I'm not sure what to do with him."

"Is he still bugging you about getting back together?" Evanna asks.

I shake my head. "No he actually stopped that a couple of weeks ago. I just don't know if I can be in the same room as him and not want to rip his head off right now," I admit to her.

"I get it. I do. Besides, I think he's crazy! I mean everyone knows you are the hottest thing in town. I mean if you're going to cheat and throw away a relationship shouldn't it be a requirement that you at least upgrade?"

I laugh, leave it to Evanna to make me laugh at the situation that has caused me the most pain lately. "If only it worked like that."

"Well, it totally should but anyways I say we go and have some fun. Besides you were right, your ass does look great in those jeans and I'm sure Jakob will be kicking himself once he sees you again since you've been avoiding him," she adds.

"I haven't been avoiding him," I lie.

Evanna is busy texting on her phone so I think the subject is done but then she looks up and smiles. "Great! Then you won't mind that I just told Ty that we'd be there in a bit."

I grimace then realize that Evanna and Ty have been spending a lot of time talking lately. "So, what about you?"

"What about me?" she asks.

Oh, this is going to be good. Any time Evanna tries to deflect you know she's got it bad. "You and Ty?"

"There is no me and Ty. I just want to go have some fun and show off this awesome second hand dress I found. It'd be a tragedy for no one to see it." She stands up and collects her plate. I follow her but with every step I take there is dread filling the pit of my stomach. If tonight can go smoothly then maybe Evanna will be satisfied for a while.

As we pull up cars are everywhere. "Are you ready?" Evanna asks.

"No time like now, right?" I tell her as I climb out of the car and follow behind her. I'm sure I should seize the moment or something like that but right now I just want to go back and hide. We open the door and all I can think is here goes nothing.

Two

Sutton

I wake up to a splitting headache. The stench of alcohol still hangs in the air and I'm stripped down to my bra and underwear which is not what I normally wear to bed. I don't recall much from last night after we arrived at Jakob's. I roll over and see a bottle of water and two white pills lying on my nightstand. I reach over and grab them. The door opens and Evanna appears. "How do you feel?"

I give her the best 'are you kidding me?' look I can muster. "Like hell, thanks for asking."

"I figured you did but I didn't want to assume things with my optimistic self."

I sigh and scrub my hands over my face and attempt to comb through the matted bed head I'm currently rocking. "I deserve that."

"Yeah, you do but that's beside the point." Evanna comes over and hands me a brush before taking a seat on the bed. "You want to tell me why you decided last night was a good night to let it all go and get beyond drunk? I mean aside from the fact that it's a really dumb decision, not to mention dangerous."

"I know, I know. I just didn't want to be at Jakob's and I think that I thought the alcohol was making it easier." I give her the best puppy dog eyes I can muster.

Evanna shakes her head. "Why didn't you just tell me that you didn't want to go?"

I sigh. "Admitting defeat is not my strong suit. Besides I could tell you wanted to go and I think there's something going on with you and Ty and I didn't want to be the reason you didn't get to have fun."

"Ugh! What am I going to do with you?" she asks.

"Love me?" I ask with a shrug.

She laughs. "I guess so but you aren't going to love yourself too much today because you have to get ready for work. I've got breakfast making and you need a shower."

I watch as she leaves before I fall back onto my bed, only to instantly regret it the moment my head hits the pillow, my head pounds harder. Today is going to be long and rough but at least I'm off tomorrow. I rush through my shower and French braid my wet hair before throwing on a pair of jeans, work boots and simple navy blue tank. I swipe a coat of mascara and eyeliner on and I'm good to go. The smell of bacon and eggs hits me instantly. My stomach rumbles then morphs into a roll of nausea. "I'm not sure if I'm hungry or going to be sick."

Evanna looks over her shoulder and smiles. "Probably both." I open the fridge and pull out a can of Dr. Pepper and crack it open before heading to our junk in the funk cabinet as we call it. It's piled with all the things you should probably feel guilty about eating but are also sometimes necessary. I search for my little bites of heaven. Once I get my hand on the can I yank it forward and pop the top off before placing one into my mouth. Evanna makes a gagging noise. "That's disgusting. I don't know how you eat those things."

My eyes go wide. This is a discussion that we have often. "Because Pizza Pringles are little bites of heaven that you can not judge me for."

"I totally judge you for them. They're gross." Evanna starts to pile our plates with food.

I give her wide eyes. "I'm not sure how we became friends. I mean I don't know if I can trust someone who doesn't love Pizza Pringles, it's just not normal."

"Being a bit dramatic, are we?" she asks.

I shake my head. "Nope, never, not when it comes to this." I grab a Pringle and try to shove it at her. She locks her lips tight and shakes her head. I start laughing which causes her to follow behind me and before she realizes it, I've shoved the chip in her mouth.

She gives me an evil look but eventually gets the chip down. "You suck, you know that, right?" I laugh. "I'm glad you're feeling better though."

I hug her. "What would I do without you Evanna?"

"You'd probably be hungry and jobless because you'd never make it to work on time. Now, take this plate and go eat so you're not late," she tells me as she extends the plate to me. I grab it and take a seat at the tiny card table we found at the thrift store a few months ago. We needed a table where we could eat and this works.

"Do you work today?" I ask her. She nods but I don't miss the look that flashes through her eyes. There's something going on but she won't talk about it. I wish she'd just get a different job but she makes killer tips at the strip club where she waitresses so I understand but I still hate it for her. We eat in silence and once I'm done I'm out the door.

I pull up to work and head inside. The smell of oil and gas hits me instantly and it gives me the feeling of comfort. I love being a mechanic. Anything to get me near a car. Memories float in my mind, like always. Every memory I have of my father is tied to a car somehow. I may be the only female mechanic at Flemings Auto but I'm also one of the best. Sure, I get underestimated a lot but I'm used to it and it's fun to prove them wrong.

As I head inside some of the guys greet me. I clock in and slip into my work overalls before heading out to the bay where I'm working on a classic American muscle car. I love to just look at it. I slide under and get to work on the motor.

"Sutton!" I hear about an hour later. I slide out from under the car and grab my rag to wipe my hands. I head over to where Rob Fleming is standing with the guy from the races, Mr. Business card man. Instantly, my suspension goes on high alert. "He's here to see you."

I take in his appearance. He's ditched the suit from last night. Today it's just jeans, a ball cap and a Revv-It racing team t-shirt. "Sutton Pierce, I'm Tucker Armstrong. I'm currently the crew chief and temporary scout for Revv-It Racing Team. Have you heard of it?"

"Can't say that I have," I tell him. I watch his every move to try and figure out if he has an ulterior motive but I can't find one yet.

He nods, "Do you follow Indy racing?"

"Nope. I can't even say I've watched a race," I admit, giving him an apologetic smile.

He waves off my nonverbal apology. "It's not as followed as Nascar but it makes for some damn good racing. Anyways, I'm looking for a new racer to join our team and when I saw you...well, I knew you were perfect."

I kind of laugh, half of it shock that this actually seems pretty legit and the other half just finds this funny. "No offense Mr. Armstrong but I'm sure there is a more formal way to recruit a racer. One that has actually trained for your track. I'm just an illegal street racing mechanic trying to make ends meet."

"You're right. There is a more formal way to go about this but most of them don't have half the talent that I saw from you the other night. You've got something that most of them don't have. The majority of those racers were born with a trust fund and haven't had to work very hard for what they have. When push comes to shove I'd bet on you, not them," he tells me. His eyes hold mine. They seem kind and caring, two things I'm not used to in this world. This man, who is a complete stranger, seems to have faith in me. I can't even begin to wrap my head around that and it makes me uncomfortable.

I shake my head, dismissing the idea. "I'm not the girl you bet on."

I turn to walk away when I hear him say, "I don't believe that. The girl I saw last night in that car was worth betting on."

I turn around and study the older man with graying hair. "Why are you trying so hard right now?"

"Look, I get that this may seem odd but a couple of years ago I followed my gut. I found a kid not too different from yourself in the sense that he thought he was just a street racer. Turns out he was a hell of an Indy racer. One of the best Revv-It has ever had. All I'm asking is for you to give me a chance to show you what you could do on the track." Silence falls between us as the war of what to do wages within me. This all seems too good to be true. "What do you say Sutton?" Well, if that isn't a million-dollar question.

Three

Rathe

I sit in my car, taking a deep breath to fight off the growing panic I feel eating it's way through the core of my body. I close my eyes like I was instructed but all I see is the wall of smoke taking away all of my visibility. My next deep breath and I smell burned rubber and leaked gasoline. My chest tightens and heart beating against my rib cage. My eyes spring open. I blink rapidly trying to bring the actual view that is in front of me back into focus. I take a deep breath through my mouth and try to calm myself but the panic runs rampant through my veins like the fuel through the engine of a car.

There's a knock on the window and I jump at the sound. Panic is a bitch. It completely locks the rest of the world away and you forget that anything else exists beyond you and that tiny little demon who makes you feel like you are drowning. I forgot I was sitting in the parking lot of Revv-It Racing Team. The parking lot of my job and just beyond is a track that should be my home. I should own it yet I don't. I'm scared shitless of it. The knock on the glass of the window comes again and I look up to see Maxton, my best friend and now head mechanic. The worry lurking in his eyes snaps me out of it. "Are you okay?"

I nod and pull the keys from the ignition of my car. As I open the door Maxton steps away and I climb out. My legs feel like jell-o and my entire body is caked in a layer of sweat. "Yeah, I'm great," I tell Maxton. It's a lie and I think we both know it but it's the one thing I keep telling everyone when they ask that question. Maxton studies me, brief moments feel like an eternity before he finally nods his head.

"Well, then we should get to the track. Tucker found a new recruit and from what I've gathered from his texts they were going to get here early to do a test run and see how he feels about the situation," Maxton explains.

My heart falters. A new recruit. Another slap in my face. Another memory I can't escape. The day of the wreck Revv-It lost their top two drivers. Chris Ziglar and myself. I'm not the same racer I was before and Chris lost his life. Last season Revv-It raced a man short in honor of Chris' memory. They all held their breaths hoping I'd get back into the groove of things but I didn't. I just couldn't. Now, this season they need a winning driver and that should be me but you can't bet on me so a new recruit seems to be the way to go. I nod my head, acknowledging that I did hear Maxton but I don't trust myself enough to speak.

We make our way through the parking lot in a comfortable silence. We only speak when we stop at security and scan our badges. Before we even make it through the building I hear the rumble of the engine and my blood pumps a little faster. We exit out of the fluorescent lighting, back into the morning sunlight. I follow behind Maxton as he leads us halfway down the stands before turning down a row and taking a seat. We watch as the driver drives at a high speed, a speed I used to crave not cower from. He takes the turns easily and it's obvious he knows how to handle a car. My mind is a jumbled mess because watching this guy drive...well, he just became my biggest rival. If he becomes part of Revv-It Racing then he's definitely going to take my spot if I don't get my shit together.

On the last lap Maxton and I stand and start to head down to the pit where Tucker and the crew are waiting. "Why didn't you come in early if the rest of the crew is here?"

"It wasn't necessary. I'm your head mechanic, not his even if he does sign with Revv-It. Besides, that car has been ready to race for a long time now." Maxton gives me a look and I know he's thinking back to the day of the wreck.

I nod my head. We cross the track just as the car comes into the pits. I hate to admit it but I'm impressed by this guy's driving ability. I envy him at this moment because I used to be him. I was that driver until it was all ripped away from me. Tucker looks our way and approaches us, extending his hand for a shake. "So, what do you think?" he asks, tossing his thumb over his shoulder, back towards the driver who is now slipping out of the car.

"Good, real good," I tell him. "Where'd you find him?" I ask.

"Same place I found you," Tucker tells me.

I chuckle and scratch at the stubble coating my jaw. "Wow, you never learn do you?"

Tucker shrugs. "What's to learn? Last time I took a chance on a street racer I got exactly what I expected. He was able to transfer everything from the street to the track."

I nod and look away. This last season with my losing streak was hard. It wasn't because I don't like to lose, which I don't but the hardest part was letting Tucker down. Disappointing him was my biggest fear and it's a fear I've had to face every single race. Tucker took a chance on me. He fought for me to be a driver despite the fact that I had no track experience. He took me under his wing and taught me everything I know. Letting my fear control me and my driving has been the worst because of him. I could quit and move on but I think in some ways that giving up would disappoint him more than my losing so I stay.

We turn to the driver and follow behind Tucker as he leads us over. He yanks his helmet off and shock consumes me. Two long chocolate brown French braids fall down the back of the driver, hitting at the small of the back. When the driver turns around another wave of shock filters through me. He is a she. A devastatingly beautiful woman.

Tucker looks between us. "Rathe McCall meet Sutton Pierce, hopefully she'll be the newest member of the Revv-It Racing Team."

I'm rooted in place but thankfully Maxton remembers his manners. He steps forward and introduces himself. I watch everything unfold like I'm watching a movie, almost as if my body is here but I'm actually somewhere else. Sutton approaches me, an easy confidence in her movements. When she reaches me her blue gray eyes light up and she smirks. "Well, Rathe it looks like I'm your new rival."

Four

Sutton

When I woke up this morning, I wasn't sure if I should actually show up at the address that Tucker Armstrong had given me. A part of me was certain it had all been a very elaborate dream but then Evanna came barrelling into my bedroom and helping me find clothes and braiding my hair. It wasn't until I was heading out the door and to my car that it finally sunk in that this was really happening.

When I pulled into the parking lot of the Revv-It Racing Team track unknown nerves settled in my stomach. I was never nervous when it came to cars. They were part of my soul but suddenly this felt like unfamiliar territory and it was terrifying. Somehow, I managed to get myself out of the car and into the building. When I found Tucker the nerves calmed some. "How are you this morning? I hope the directions I gave were easy enough to follow."

I nod. "Yeah, they were great. I didn't have any trouble."

"Well, if you want to follow me, we can get right to it." Tucker leads the way through the building. I try to take it all in but in all honestly, it's overwhelming. This place is fancy compared to what I'm used to. The building smells clean and it's quiet at the moment. We make our way through a well lit tunnel like hallway. There are some other hallways that break off from this one and even a few doors. Finally, the sunlight can be seen up ahead. As we step out, I notice the stands are on either side of me. From here they look as if they reach up to the sky and the bright turquoise seats stand out in the morning sunlight. We cross over the track to the main area. There are some people there

31

but not a lot which I'm thankful for. I'm already nervous. "Okay, first we need to get you in the proper gear." He leads me to a trailer and opens the door. There are some things lying on the couch. Tucker explains each one and why they are necessary then leaves me to slip them on. I take a few moments to take a few deep breaths before heading back outside. Tucker is waiting for me and instantly leads me over to the car. It's definitely not the type of car I'm used to. Tucker and one of the mechanics, who's name I've already forgotten, tell me all the important things I might need to know. "Look, don't worry too much about it. Once you have the helmet on, we'll be able to communicate so if anything comes up just ask. I'll be with you the whole time and if for some reason the car doesn't feel right just come back into the pit."

"Okay, I can do that," I tell him. My voice comes out sounding much stronger and self-assured than I feel. I walk over to where the mechanic is standing. He helps me adjust the helmet before I slide into the car that kind of reminds me of a spaceship. It almost reminds me of The Jetsons. Damn, it had always been my favorite growing up.

"Sutton, can you hear me?" Tucker asks.

I nod before I realize I probably need to actually speak to him. "Yeah, I can hear you."

"Great, so just go ahead and leave the pit. Take your time with speed for now. You need to get a feel of the car and the track so go ahead and do a couple of laps before really letting loose." My heart pounds as I pull out of the pit area. However, the moment I hit the track it all fades away. Despite the look of the car or where the asphalt is, it's all the same for me. Racing and cars are like my second skin and I instantly feel at home once I hit the blacktop. I smile to myself but I do take Tucker's advice and do a couple of slower laps around the track. It's a much smoother drive than what I'm used to. I mean when you street race you don't have an area that's just for racing. Then there's the fact that you have to deal with the condition of the roads, potholes being a big part of it. This is like driving in a dream, only better. As I approach the line Tucker comes through the speakers. "How are you feeling Sutton?"

"Great, this is awesome," I admit. I hate to allow anyone to know how much something like this means to me because if there's one thing I've learned in my life it's that the more you enjoy something the harder it is to let go.

Tucker chuckles. "Great, then why don't you go ahead and open up on the next lap and see how that feels."

"I thought you'd never ask." As I pull away from the line and push down on the accelerator. The car eases up in speed and before I know it I'm flying around the track, taking the curves like a pro. The curves on a track were my biggest concern but you wouldn't know that right now. At this moment, I'm free. I have no worries, no past, present or future. It's just me, this car and track. It's so much more than I could have ever asked for. That scares me because if this doesn't last then my heart will be broken but I'm no stranger to that either. My mind drifts to thoughts of my father. I start to ease up on the accelerator because of it.

Tucker must notice because he comes through the speakers once more, "That was great Sutton, why don't you go ahead and come on into the pit?" I ease into the pit and come to a stop. The mechanic comes over and helps me out of the car. As I'm pulling the helmet off, I hear Tucker. When I turn around to face him my eyes are instantly drawn to one of the two guys approaching beside him. His hair is so dark it's almost black as the night sky and thick. I want to run my fingers through it just to see if it's as thick as it looks. His bone structure makes him look like he should be a model. The dark, trimmed beard gives him a mysterious feeling but add that with the sunglasses that conceal his eyes and I have no idea what I'm thinking, all I know is that I'm a jumbled mess. My heart slams around inside my chest, beating erratically like the wings of a hummingbird. Tucker looks between us. "Rathe McCall meet Sutton Pierce, hopefully she'll be the newest member of the Revv-It Racing Team."

Rathe makes no move towards me. The man standing beside him with strawberry blonde hair steps forward and introduces himself. "I'm Maxton Wilson, Rathe's head mechanic." I nod and shake his hand.

I approach Rathe, drawn to him like a moth to a flame, I feel this undeniable pull towards him. My movements feel awkward and out of sync but I'm praying that doesn't show. I study him up close before giving him my signature smirk. "Well, Rathe it looks like I'm your new rival." He stands there, intensely staring at me. I can feel it through his sunglasses. That stare heats my skin but I don't give it away. I wait for a reply but he gives me nothing so I turn to Tucker and smile.

"Well, why don't you go change and then we can get down to the numbers," Tucker tells me.

"Sounds great." I look over my shoulder at Rathe and Maxton. "It was great meeting you boys." I walk away hoping that I don't look as silly as I feel right now. Rathe McCall just knocked my world off of it's axis and I'm not sure how to fix it.

Five

Sutton

I spend some extra time in the trailer because my heart still hasn't returned to normal. It's ridiculous that I can feel...whatever the hell this is for some guy that didn't even speak to me. I mean sure he was good looking but I'm around good looking people a lot. I should not have been so bothered by him. I shake my head in an attempt to clear it. It must have been the run in with Jakob the other night that has me so wound up. When I open the door, I easily spot Tucker with Rathe, Maxton and the other mechanic whose name I still can't seem to remember. As I make my way to them, I take in the beautiful morning and allow myself to accept this for what it is...a possibility. A hopeful possibility and despite how scary that is I know it's going to be so hard to pass up. Tucker smiles and as I approach and he steps away from the guys. "Do you want to take a walk?" he asks, motioning back to the track. I just nod my head in reply because I'm not sure what to say right now. We've been walking in silence for a few moments before Tucker asks, "What got you interested in cars and racing?"

I shrug as I dig my hands into the back pockets of my jeans. "My dad. He was always into cars. It's the main thing I remember about him. It used to be us against the world."

"Oh, I'm sorry. I didn't realize he had passed." Tucker gives me a sympathetic smile.

The truth and lies wage a war on my tongue. Taking a deep breath I let the truth spill out. "I don't know if he has. To be honest I don't know much about him now. My dad did whatever he could to provide for me but it led him to some questionable

35

situations and in the long run he got busted and last I knew he was being carted off to jail."

Tucker studies me but I keep my eyes trained directly ahead. I know what I'll see if I look into his eyes. It'll be sympathy and pity, those are two things I don't need right now. I've learned over the years to avoid eye contact with most people because they really are doorways into our souls. I feel like my secrets will all be laid out in the open if I look him in the eye now. "What about your mom?" he finally asks. He probably doesn't even notice it but his voice is slightly lower with an edge of softness to it now that he knows a piece about my past.

I scoff. "I don't know. She was never around. My dad didn't talk about her so I don't know if she just left or if she died. I always meant to ask him but I was so young and still trying to process what I could...and, I don't know, the next thing I knew CPS was rushing in and tearing my world apart. I was shoved into foster care, met Evanna and the rest is history."

"Was she in foster care too?"

I shake my head. "No, she was my next door neighbor. Her mom was a single mother and working as a stripper to feed the five mouths she had. Evanna was the youngest and also the quietest. We ended up in the same class and some damn ogre was picking on her." I stop because Tucker bursts out laughing. I give him a questioning look.

He waves his hands in apology. "I'm sorry. It's just when you said ogre I immediately pictured Shrek."

I laugh. "Well, then you got the picture only she wasn't nice at all. Anyways, Evanna wouldn't stand up for herself so I stood up for her. We became best friends after that."

Tucker and I continue to walk, the silence between us thick with tension. I can tell he has more questions but I'm not sure how many more answers I have for him. I've already told him more than I ever tell anyone. I mean even Jakob doesn't know everything I just told Tucker. This is uncharted territory for me and I'm not liking it much at the moment. "Sutton, what you did on the track today was really good. You have huge potential and I think that you should give this a shot. You'd make some great money even being a rookie and the crowd will love you."

"I don't race for the crowd."

"Okay, then forget that they're there. Is this something you want to do?" he asks. I stop and turn to face him, crossing my arms over my chest. The sun is nearly blinding where it sits behind him but then it almost gives him a heavenly glow. It makes it hard to decide if he's my saving grace, guardian angel or a devil in disguise. I finally shrug because I don't know how to answer that question. "Why do you race Sutton?"

I sigh and look away. That's been a question I've been asked so many times since I first started driving. "I don't know. It's the one thing I know I'm good at. It also reminds me of my dad but I also know that Indy racing is not something he'd be into. He was all about American muscle and foreign imports, modifications and NOS. This wouldn't have been something he'd support."

"Does that matter?" Tucker raises his eyebrows along with the verbal question.

I wish I could say that it doesn't matter but at the end of the day I think every child just wants approval from their parents. I'm no different in that aspect despite the years that I've fended for myself. I stare at the track, lost in thought. My skin burns from the unforgiving sun but still I don't move.

"Look, you have a great opportunity here, one I think you'd be crazy to let pass you by. I obviously can't tell you what to do but I can tell you this, I think you race for another reason. I think it gives you purpose in a life where you haven't had a lot of that. I think it gives you fleeting moments where it can be you and your dad against the world because when you slide behind the wheel of a car, he's there with you. You say he wouldn't approve of this type of racing but let me tell you something Sutton, it's all racing at the end of the day. It's all cars, engines, fuel and speed. It doesn't matter if it's on a track, on the street or what kind of car you're doing it in, it's still racing."

I stare at Tucker. My mouth is basically on the ground. No one has ever put my feelings into words, myself included but somehow this stranger just hit the nail on the head. I swallow past the lump of emotion in my throat. "Can I think about it?"

Tucker nods. "I can give you forty-eight hours. After that, though, I'll have to look elsewhere. I need someone in that car, ready to train and ready to win and I need that driver soon so I can get them ready before the race season."

"Okay," I reply before turning around and walking away. I have no clue what the hell I'm going to do now.

Six

Rathe

This can't be my life right now. I mean seriously, it just can't be. Why in the hell would Tucker go out and recruit another street racer for Revv-It? Another question, why her? It's so obvious that she doesn't belong on this track that I think I may have been shocked into silence earlier. I'll give Sutton credit though she's got some audacity. I mean stepping up to me and making that comment about rivals. I shake my head as I think about it now. It was ridiculous and the moment I should have put her in her place but instead I stood there silent and looking dumb.

I'm pacing in the trailer where her lavender scent still lingers, only pissing me off more. I mean, seriously? They let her use my trailer. Why couldn't she change in the bathrooms? I mean maybe she's just too good for all that. She's probably one of the silver spoon princess types. All beautiful with curves like a track, just enough to drive us mad. Damn it! Why can't I stop thinking about her?

The knock on the door nearly makes me jump out of my skin. Maxton appears once the door is open. "Hey, you coming to practice or what?" I nod my head but Maxton doesn't let it die there. He knows me well, too well sometimes because he can tell by looking at me that something is bugging me. He'll either figure it out on his own or he'll pester the shit out of me until I tell him. "What's going on man?"

"Nothing, I'm just having an off day." I look away and begin to pace once more.

I hear the door click as it shuts and for a moment, I take a deep breath, assuming that Maxton left me to dwell on my own but as

39

I turn around to pace back he's standing there. Maxton's face is serious, his stance rigid and his eyes are locked on me like he means business. He almost looks like a statue and the laughter that bubbles up out of my chest and exits my mouth, surprises us both. After a moment of laughing Maxton asks, "Should I be worried about you Rathe?" I shake my head, instantly dismissing the idea. "Look, I know we don't talk about the wreck really but if you need to talk about it, I'm here."

"I know that but there's just not anything to talk about when it comes to that situation," I tell him, giving him the best smile I can muster.

By the look on his face it's either not enough or not believable. "There's definitely something to talk about. I mean you can act like it wasn't a big deal or that it didn't happen but it was a big deal and it did happen. Chris died that day along with two other racers. You were lucky to get out of that mess alive. I don't think you're dealing with it Rathe."

The sarcastic laugh and shake of my head has become my go-to defense mechanism. "That's funny. I didn't think you were a damn therapist. Oh! That's right, you aren't. Why don't you stop trying to psychoanalyze me and get your ass under the hood of my car? That's what your pay grade gets you."

Maxton's eyes flash with hurt instantly turning my tongue to acid as the words I just spat out linger between us. The hurt morphs into disappointment and I'm not sure which is worse. Maxton snorts. "And you say you're fine…" His statement falls between us for a moment before he turns and leaves the trailer, the door slamming shut behind him.

I turn around and punch the wall because I just became the biggest jackass of all.

****

I wish I could say that my test runs had gone well but they didn't. I was angry with myself for talking to Maxton the way I did. He is my best friend and he's always had my back. I shouldn't have done that to him. I was also angry at Tucker. Even though I knew I had no right to be angry at him, I was. Tucker had a job to do and he was simply doing it. It wasn't his fault that I couldn't seem to get my shit together and be the driver I was my first race season on the track. Revv-It Racing needed some wins in the upcoming season and I wasn't the one to bet money on now days. The wreck had destroyed more than my car that day.

When I exit the trailer, I scan the area, looking for Maxton, I need to apologize. I don't see him anywhere so I stop and ask a couple of the crew but they tell me he had left right after he ran the check through on the car. I know I upset him, even hurt his feelings but I am trying to make it right. Now, I'll have to wait until lunch while Ryann watches me apologize. She is going to eat that up. There is nothing she finds more entertaining than watching me try to apologize. Apologizing is not my strong suit. It never has been and to be honest who was good at apologizing? I mean who wants to admit they were wrong?

Slipping on my sunglasses I wave goodbye to the security guards sitting at the gates. I head out to my truck and climb inside. Grabbing my phone I text Ryann to let her know I'm on my way but I might be a little late. You can never know what kind of traffic you'll hit during this time of the day. She doesn't reply the whole way to the restaurant which isn't a good sign. Ryann probably already knows what I said to Maxton and she's pissed about it, I'm sure. She's the other third of our trio and highly protective over both of us, even if that means she's upset with one of us.

I cut the engine and hop out of the car. Ryann is easy to spot. Her yellow sundress outshines everything around us. It's so bright in contrast to her raven colored hair which is down and in loose curls. Her hazel eyes find mine and she glares as I approach. When she stands, I notice she's a little taller and it's not just because she's wearing sky high wedges, it's the straightening of her spine and squaring her shoulders, her preparation for battle with me. She's going to let me have it. "You look stunning," I tell her.

She scoffs and rolls her eyes as I lean in and pull her into a quick embrace. Normally, Ryann is one of the most affectionate people I know but right now she's stiff as a board. She's clearly more upset than I anticipated, not that I blame her. "Well, at least you can be nice to someone or did you finally get that stick out of your ass."

Ryann sits back in her seat, her eyes unwavering while she waits for my answer. I sigh and take a seat. "I know I was a jackass to Maxton today and he didn't deserve it."

"You're damn right he didn't. None of us are deserving of your attitude lately." Ryann looks away and studies the people on the sidewalk next to the outdoor seating she has chosen for us today.

"I'm sorry Ryann. I really am." I hope she can hear the sincerity in my voice because I am sorry. I don't want to hurt her, Maxton or my family but sometimes I'm just so lost in my own head with no way out. My aggression comes out verbally when I talk to them.

Ryann takes a deep breath before turning back to face me. Her eyes swim with moisture and emotion. "I know that Rathe. I know you but I can't pretend that I don't notice the changes in you since the accident. I also can't pretend to understand what you went through or how you feel now but I do know that you are letting the fear win and that's a damn shame."

Her words shock me but then again Ryann has never been one to sugar coat something to ease your feelings. She's in your face, to the point and completely honest. My mind wanders to Sutton and I know that her and Ryann would get along just fine. The waiter appears and we order our food. "So, Revv-It might have found it's new rookie driver."

"Maxton mentioned that but I didn't get any details from his grumpy ass. So, you need to spill."

I chuckle. "Well, she's a woman."

Ryann rolls her eyes at my response. "Please, don't turn into one of those sexist men now. You know damn good and well a woman can race just as good as any man if she wants."

I hold up my hands in defense. "I didn't mean anything by it. It was just the first thing I noticed about her."

She smirks before taking a drink of her water. "Of course, it was. So did you see her race and was she any good?"

"We caught her laps on the track and yeah she's got some talent there. She took the curves with ease, didn't let up on the accelerator too soon and she's confident as hell so that'll help her especially in the male dominated sport. She'll need the thick skin that confidence will provide." I think back to Sutton now that I've had time to cool down and realize that she was in fact a damn good driver but under that confidence was an uncertainty I noticed in the depths of her eyes and it made me curious.

"Well, I hope she joins the team and I hope she gives you a run for your money because you need a challenge," Ryann tells me as she sticks her tongue out at me.

"Yeah, yeah, eat your damn food," I tell her as the waiter appears with our plates but her words linger. Maybe, a challenge is what I need to get me to kick my ass into gear. Maybe, the rival of Sutton will be exactly what I need to truly race again.

Seven

Sutton

I barrel through the door of our apartment with my arms full of take out. I figured if I had to make some big life decisions then I need pizza, wings, pasta and Evanna to do it. "Honey, I'm home," I call out.

Evanna appears in the doorway of her room, takes one look at my arms which are just about to give out and darts over to take some of my load. "You know I would have come down to help you with some of this right?"

I shrug. "Yeah, but I managed pretty well on my own until I had to open the door."

Evanna shakes her head. "Okay there, Miss Independent, by the looks of all this junk food we are either celebrating, which I hope we are, or we are making big decisions, so which is it?"

I laugh as I place the stuff still in my arms on the kitchen counter. "Well, it's possible that you know me too well."

"Completely possible, also completely true but beyond the point. Also, don't think I don't know that you're trying to change the subject right now by having this discussion. So, are we celebrating or making decisions?" Evanna stares me down from across the small kitchen island until I start to squirm. When she raises her eyebrow I cave.

"Fine, we're making decisions."

Evanna rolls her eyes, true to her style. "Then that's easy, you take the job if they offer it to you. You'd be crazy not to but I would just like it noted that I told you this was legit."

I sigh and hop onto the counter to sit. "Yes, you did. I'm sorry for doubting you and your mad skills." Evanna spins and does a curtsey. "But you know making this decision is not that easy."

Evanna shakes her head at my words. "Please, tell me which part is so difficult about this decision because I'm just not seeing it." I sigh and look away but I can feel her presence as she moves across the kitchen despite the fact that she's so quiet when she moves. "Sutton, what's really holding you up?"

That was the million dollar question and one that I had the answer to but I had yet to say it out loud to anyone. Evanna would probably be the first person I'd tell when I'm ready but I'm not there. I may never be. I shrug. "I don't know. You know me. I worry about every little thing, every little change."

"Yeah, you do but there is more to this and I know it. If you don't want to talk about it you know you can just tell me that, right?"

I nod my head after a few moments. "I'm just not sure how to talk about it yet."

"Okay, that's fine. I'm here when you want to but for the record you deserve this opportunity and I think you'd be crazy not to take it. You're so talented and this is basically a once in a lifetime chance." Evanna opens the wing box and grabs one before hopping onto the kitchen island. "So, you do what you have to do and I support you no matter what."

"Thanks," I tell her as I reach over and grab a wing as well. I really am lucky to have her to call my friend because I know that no matter what she has my back and that's not an easy thing to come by. Evanna looks up and smirks. "What?"

"So, have you met Rathe McCall?"

Her question throws me for a loop because I can't even begin to figure out how she knows anything about Rathe McCall. Then there's the odd fact that I'm overly attracted to him for no reason at all. "What do you know about Rathe McCall?"

She smiles. "A lot more than you think. I may have spent my day doing some down and dirty research on your competition in case you take this job. One, I found that the Indy racers are either hot as hell or way too old for us. Two, Colton Donavan and Rathe McCall are on the top of mine and every other females' list. They are seriously hot. Also, Rathe will be your teammate if you race for Revv-It Racing, which I think you should."

I shake my head because I should have known she'd instantly get to work on digging up every last bit of information she could find on all things Indy racing. That's just how Evanna is. She's always been a planner. "I met Rathe," I admit quietly and watch as her eyes go wide.

Evanna jumps off the kitchen island and comes to stand in front of me. "Way to hold back...that should have been one of the first things out of your mouth when you walked through that door. I mean seriously! How hot is he in person?"

I shrug. I'm trying to play like I don't care, act nonchalant but I know that Evanna probably sees right through it. "He's okay. I met him and his head mechanic, Maxton."

She scoffs at my reaction. "He's okay? What? Were you blind at this particular moment in time?"

I laugh. "No, I just don't happen to think Rathe McCall is all that great. His mechanic was nice though."

"You're impossible."

I laugh. "Why? Because I don't find Rathe McCall the irresistible ladies' man that the tabloids make him out to be?" Shrugging I reach for a soda and open the can, taking a long drink.

Evanna laughs and shakes her head. "No, because you totally find him irresistible but won't admit it."

"I do not," I tell her. My tone is harsh and I know I've given it all away.

Her head falls back in laughter. "You totally do! I knew it. I knew the moment I saw his pictures online that you would be daydreaming about him while denying it to the ends of the earth."

"You don't know what you're talking about." I make it a point to hop off the counter and busy myself with making a plate of food.

"I call bullshit! You totally know what I'm talking about you just won't admit to it because that's what you do. You act all badass and indifferent but really you care more than anyone I know. Rathe got under your skin and you aren't sure what to make of it now." I look over my shoulder at her, eyes narrowed and she smirks at me. "I'm right, aren't I?"

"No, you aren't."

"Yes, I am," she replies, her voice triumphant. "Deny it all you want but you like him."

"It's kind of hard to like someone who never acknowledges your existence and treats you as if you don't belong on the same track as him. Rathe McCall is just another spoiled, rich brat who thinks he's above everyone else. He might be hot but his attitude is ugly," I rant.

Evanna gives me a sad smile. "I'm sorry. I really thought he might be different. He seemed so friendly and outgoing in his interview videos."

I shrug. "It doesn't matter. It's just who he is. The interview videos are probably just for show."

Evanna walks over to me, a wicked smile on her face. "You know what this all means, don't you?" I shake my head as my eyebrows pull together in confusion. "You have to take this job and you have to race him. You have to win and you have to knock him off his high and mighty pedestal."

"I don't know about all that." I laugh at the picture she paints but she isn't necessarily wrong.

"Just wait and see," she winks before grabbing a plate and piling it with food. I laugh because I have no idea where she puts it. As I'm standing there though my thoughts go back to Rathe and then Evanna's words. Her words don't make the worst idea ever. They've piqued my curiosity. Maybe, she's right. Maybe, I need to step up and knock him off his stool and show him what real driving looks like. We may be on the same team but we are definitely going to end up rivals.

Eight

Sutton

Sleep doesn't come easily that night. Everything that happened throughout the day plays back through my mind in slow motion. I try everything from warm milk to counting sheep yet I stayed awake staring at my ceiling. As soon as the sun started to break through the blinds covering my bedroom window I crawled out of bed and got ready for the day. Somewhere in the sleepless night I had come to my decision. It was the only one I could make. I knew it all along but I fought against it because I'm afraid of hurting others but in the end this is my life and I have to do what makes me happy. I leave a note on the fridge for Evanna and sneak out of the apartment. I take a long drive to clear my head and heart, both are so conflicted at the moment.

My dad always said to think with your head first but to follow your heart. There's a problem with that. Your heart is a flawed organ in your body. It'll hide it's true desires in fear of getting hurt or hurting others. It can be mischievous and difficult. It can build a wall that would rival the Great wall of China. The heart can master the game of hide and seek. It often wears a mask to protect itself and leaves your entire soul in conflict. Your head and heart could want the same thing but the heart might mislead you. It might lie to you thinking that it's doing the right thing but it's wrong. My head and heart have wanted the same thing all along but I was being played by my heart and now it's time to find the truth within it.

I roll down the windows of my beat up Camaro and turn the music up. The good ol' 90s rock blasting through my speakers. I was never one to keep up with music of my time. I always loved the raw emotion of the 90s rock. The lyrics could move me and when the lyrics failed the music didn't. Right now, Dave Matthews Band is my anthem and it's exactly what I need. As the Revv-It Racing track comes into view one of my all time favorite songs comes on and I know I'm making the right decision.

I notice a couple of cars already in the parking lot. Some people get here really early I think to myself as I park in a space. As I sit there letting the song finish I notice Rathe climb out of a truck across from me. I watch as he moves so gracefully. Most guys I know don't move like him. He's beautiful to watch and I can only imagine how he must drive a car. I'm curious to see him in action. I take these moments to watch him even though I shouldn't. I'm sure it isn't going to help my thoughts stay away from him but something about how he moves draws me in. Who am I kidding? It almost seems like everything he does draws me in. It's ridiculous but he's devastatingly handsome and he moves with such purpose that it's hard to take your eyes away from him. No wonder he was such a hit his rookie year.

Once he reaches the building and scans his badge through, I pull myself out of the car and make my way up to the front. As I approach, I realize I have no badge to get me inside and I didn't spot Tucker's car in the parking lot yet. I really should have thought this through better. However, as soon as the security guard sitting at the door spots me he waves. Maybe, luck is on my side because he was also here yesterday. I walk over and notice his name tag says Patrick. "Good morning Patrick."

Patrick is an older man that's a little on the heavier side. He almost reminds me of Kevin James. His eyebrows pull together in confusion. "How'd you know my name?" I point to the area where his name tag sits on his uniform. "Oh yeah, I forget about that."

"It's all part of the uniform, right?" I tease him with a shrug.

He nods his head. "Are you here to see Tucker Miss Pierce?"

"Please, call me Sutton and yes. Is he here yet?"

"No ma'am, but he should be here within the next twenty minutes. He's a very scheduled man. He's rarely late. If you want you go on ahead and wait for him in the stands," Patrick tells me as he motions back towards the track.

I debate on accepting his offer. Patrick seems like a nice guy and I don't want to get him in any trouble. "Are you sure?"

Patrick chuckles. "Don't you worry about me. I've been around here so long that I'm practically a fixture nowadays. They couldn't get rid of me if they tried. You go on ahead," he encourages me as he unlocks the gate.

I smile and move through the gate. I turn back around to Patrick. "Thank you."

"Anytime Sutton." His big smile is friendly and causes the corners of his eyes to crinkle.

My head tilts to the side with curiosity. "How'd you know my name?"

"Tucker told me yesterday."

His answer means that he remembered my name and it pulls at my heart. I mean to most it probably seems silly to get emotional over someone remembering something as insignificant as your name but to someone who was marked as forgotten by everyone in her life and a system that was meant to provide her with something more, it means the world. "Thank you, Patrick."

Patrick nods his head. "I hope I get to see a lot of you around here Sutton. You sure do brighten up this place."

"I'll see what I can do about that." As I turn away, I hear him whistling the theme song to Andy Griffith and it settles my nerves instantly. It's funny how some people can turn your whole day around.

The place is eerily quiet as I walk through the empty halls. I try to picture it packed with people, the air crackling with excitement on a race day but for some reason I can only picture it like this. When I reach the stands, I take a seat and study the track. From the stands the track looks huge. The immensity of it is almost overwhelming but when I was down there, behind the wheel of the car and racing around it, well it felt so small in comparison. I sit back and watch as Rathe walks out to his car and gets into place.

I'm intrigued to watch him. He pulls out of the pit without any issues. He accelerates quickly and moves like he owns the track which he basically does...or did at least. I watch him carefully because the driver I'm seeing right now should be winning races not losing. On his sixth lap around the second curve something in the air shifts. Rathe suddenly backs off from his aggressive speed. I try to watch the car to see if it's having an issue but I don't notice anything. I scan the area where the crew are standing, then the stand where Maxton is sitting with a headset on. He's shaking his head. Apparently, this is why Rathe is losing.

"It's a damn shame how badly the wreck messed with his head." Tucker startles me and I nearly jump out of my seat. "I'm sorry," he says with a chuckle. "I didn't mean to scare you."

"It's okay, I was just wrapped up watching the track and didn't hear you come up." I stand up and turn to face him. His eyes are expectant.

"Well, I'm hoping that since you're here in person that means that you are going to be my new driver because if you are declining my offer you could have broken my heart over a call or text."

I sigh and run a hand through my hair while I look back to the track. I already know what I'm going to do. I just need to get my head and heart to both accept it. When I turn back to Tucker, I know he's worried I'm going to decline. I can tell by the crease forming between his eyebrows. I take a deep breath and release it. "I'm in," I tell him quietly. His face lights up like the sky on the fourth of July. He claps his hands and smiles at me.

"You won't regret this Sutton." I nod my head unable to find any words but I hope he's right.

Nine

Rathe

When I woke up this morning I was determined. My mind was clear and set. Anxiety just seemed like another term I often heard thrown about on TV or on the radio. It didn't exist within the confines of my body. It was like I had never suffered from anxiety or a panic attack before. I felt amazing. I felt like the old me. The version of me that won races, took chances and worried about the consequences later. It was early but I got dressed and went for a run anyways. It felt good. The music of Falling in Reverse blaring into my ears, energizing my body for the day ahead. I had it planned out. Once I arrived at the track I would apologize profusely to Maxton before getting into my car and driving like I haven't driven in over a year. In my mind it was so clear and simple. It's funny how things rarely worked out that way.

However, my mood changed on my way to the track. As soon as I pulled into the parking lot my determination went out the window. My chest tightened. There I was again, this new weak version of myself. A failure that wasn't able to keep his shit together anymore. I was supposed to be strong but I was far from it. Somehow, I managed to pull myself from my truck and as I did I noticed my newest possible rival sitting across from me. I knew that Tucker said he was waiting for an answer from her. Selfishly, I had hoped she'd say no but surely, she wasn't so cruel as to show up and deliver that blow to Tucker's face. If I had to guess I'd say I was about to become teammates with little miss race princess.

It was ridiculous how good she was yesterday. I would have bet money she grew up in the Indy world but Tucker swears that's not true. I'm still not sure I buy it. Maybe, she's just playing everyone. Who knows? Frustration ebbs it's way through my body. I barely acknowledge Patrick as I scan my badge. He's always been incredibly friendly but I don't have it in me right now to make small talk. My mood has soured and self-loathing is consuming me. I hate this version of me but I can't seem to keep him buried.

I spot Maxton as soon as I make it to the shop portion of the building. Detouring from my trailer I head towards Maxton. He must spot me from the corner of his eye because he turns on his heels and speed walks into his office, as if I won't follow him there. I knock on the open door. He looks up and it's as if you can see his mood plummet as quickly as mine did when I pulled up to the track. "Can I help you Mr. McCall?"

"Ouch, that stings, not that I don't deserve it after yesterday but still..." I tell him. Maxton and I stare at each other. The tension in the air is thick, it's almost as if you can see it. He raises his eyebrows in question after a few moments of silence. I open my mouth only to have words fail me so I close it back.

Maxton sharply nods once. "Well, if there's nothing I can do for you then I need to get back to making sure your car is ready for the test run today. I mean that is my pay grade and all."

"Damn it, Max. I'm sorry, okay! I'm sorry! I was an ass to you because I was upset with myself and the new driver and I took it out on you because I could. It wasn't fair or right and I'm sorry," I tell him. I throw my hands up in surrender.

Silence falls between us once more but the tension is less this time. "Rathe, I know you're stressed right now. I know this new driver situation isn't ideal with your last season stats but I can't help that. My job is to make sure that the car is ready and it is. My job is to make sure I guide your blind spots and I do. My job is to make sure that my best friend doesn't ruin his career over a wreck but I can only do so much for that. You have to meet me halfway here."

"It wasn't just a wreck," I say harshly. People are always trying to downplay it and I hate that. People died that day. I could have been one of them, yet they think that shouldn't mess with my head.

Maxton rounds his desk. "But it was just a wreck."

"People died! How can you say that?"

He shakes his head. "Every time you've gotten into that car and drove whatever track for whichever race there's been a possibility of a wreck, of someone losing their life. That's part of this sport that you decided to be part of. You have to figure out a way to handle this shit or it's going to handle you. It's going to cost you everything. I'm doing everything I can." I advert my eyes but nod my head so he knows I hear him. "I love you man. You're like a brother to me but for the record if you ever talk to me like you did yesterday, I'm done. I'll wash my hands and walk away. I can work anywhere and I won't be talked to like that again."

"I won't do it again." As I make my way back to the trailer to put on my driving gear, I can't help but feel a little lost in thought. Once I've changed, I stop by the door to grab a couple of Sour Patch Kids before heading outside. I cross the track to my car. I can feel the anxiety start to rise as I slip the helmet on and secure it. I try to shake the feeling off but it's only growing stronger with each breath I take.

Maxton appears in front of me, tapping my helmet to pull me back to reality. "Just breathe man." I nod my head and take some deep calming breaths. "You've got this." Maxton holds my eyes, calm and steady until I feel the anxiety start to drift back to bay.

I climb into the car and pull out to the start line on the track. "Okay, remember it's just a test drive. Take your time on the first couple of laps but then let her rip once you're ready."

"Got it," I reply.

I hear a little static on the other end of the speakers. "Okay, whenever you're ready."

I ease away from the start line. I take the first couple of laps at a normal speed, nothing too crazy just in case the car has some kinks that need to be worked out still but on the third lap I really start to accelerate. The car moves with ease, it takes the curves smoothly and from what I can tell it's in the best shape it's ever been. I continue to accelerate my speed until the second curve on the sixth lap. Suddenly, it all hits me. The soul crushing anxiety. Memories flood my reality out. I see nothing but smoke, smell nothing but gasoline and burned rubber from the tires desperately seeking traction. I see Chris' car slam into the wall before flipping over just as something from the side of my eye comes racing towards me. I slow the car to a school zone speed. I know this isn't real but it feels real. Sweat soaks my skin, running into my eyes, burning them as if the smoke really is here. My lungs constrict begging for fresh oxygen that I can't seem to find.

"Rathe!" I can hear Maxton's voice but it sounds so far away, so muffled. The only thing I hear is the pounding of my blood rushing through my ears. I try every exercise that has been taught to me since the wreck but nothing is working. The car starts to pull to the right, towards the wall, or maybe it's me causing that. "Rathe! Damn it man!"

"There's something wrong with that car," I whisper. My voice is weak just like I feel.

"No, there isn't. You're letting up on the gas. You're panicking Rathe," Maxton's voice is calm and collected.

I shake my head. "No, it's not right, something is wrong." I come to a stop and hang my head. This isn't happening. I yank the helmet off my head and let the wind hit my face. The first deep breath feels like heaven. I look around the track and see Maxton coming towards me. "There's something wrong with the car."

He gives me a sad look. "It's not the car Rathe."

I pace away from him as anger boils in my blood. He's right. I know it, he knows it, this whole damn track knows it. I'm supposed to be on top of the world right now. I should have owned the track last season. I should be the name the other drivers are in awe and fear of. Instead, I'm the pathetic loser who suffers from crippling anxiety and panic attacks now after being involved in one wreck. The worst part is Max was right. I knew the minute I signed the line on the contract that wrecks were a likely consequence. They didn't scare me then but they do now. None of it makes sense. I just want to get in the car and drive like I'm meant to. I turn towards the wall of the track and hurl my helmet towards it. I watch as it arches in the air before slamming into the wall and scattering into pieces just like the day of the wreck, just like my career now.

Ten

Sutton

As I leave the office, I take a deep breath. I feel this need to pinch myself because there is no way that this is my life. I did not just sign a contract to become an Indy race car driver for Revv-It Racing Team. That's just not possible. This feels like one of those Cinderella stories that I've never believed in. Those types of things only happened in the movies or books, not in real life and definitely not to me. When I get onto the elevator and head down to the main level to get my security badge created, I'm on cloud nine. My phone alerts me of a text and as soon as I step out of the elevator, I dial Evanna. "You're a sneaky bitch. You better have your ass at that track, signing some major contract to race professionally. If you aren't doing exactly that I'm disowning you as of this moment."

I laugh. "Always so dramatic. I'm telling you that you should really consider acting."

"Stop deflecting! Stop changing the subject and fess the hell up!"

"Easy killer. I just signed my three year contract. If my first season goes well then, I might get a raise the next season. It all depends on stats but even without a raise it's more money than either of us as ever seen combined. We're definitely getting a better place, one in a better part of town," I explain to her.

Evanna sighs on the other end of the line. I know she's going to protest. "Look, I love you for always looking after me but you seriously don't have to. You should get yourself a really awesome place. I can stay here and get a new roommate. I'll be fine."

Evanna has always been this super kind and very sensitive person. From the moment we met I knew she might have grown up in a rough home and neighborhood but she still had this optimistic outlook on life. She had this light in her eyes that hadn't been killed out yet so I made it my point to protect her. She's like my little sister. I laugh into the phone. "You're funny. You're my best friend and I don't intend on sharing you. Sorry, I'm an only child, well at least as far as I know, but the point is that only children don't share well so you can either help me find us an awesome new place, one that accepts pets so we can get that damn dog you've always wanted or we can continue to live in the ghetto. Your choice?"

"Wow, you officially become a big shot Indy race car driver and all of a sudden you're bossy," she teases.

I scoff. "I'm always bossy."

"This is true."

"Hey!" I exclaim while laughing. The line goes quiet. "Look, in case I haven't said it, thank you for believing in me and pushing me to give this a real shot."

"That's what friends are for," she tells me quietly. "So, do you want an apartment, house or condo?"

"Nothing too big or crazy, just something in a decent part of town."

"I'll start looking," she admits.

"Good, now I'm going to finish up all the stuff I have to do here but tonight we are going to celebrate, Evanna and Sutton style!"

"So...pizza, wings, soda and probably watch In the Dark so we can swoon over Casey Deidrick, right?" she asks.

I laugh with her. "Of course."

"See you later and good luck at work!" Evanna disconnects the call and her parting words hit me in the gut. Work? Is it truly possible that this is now my job. I mean this is seriously a dream come true. It's not a dream I ever truly considered for myself but it's still a dream come true. I'm not sure what to make of this now that the idea has hit me. Then it reminds me that I'll have to quit my job at the shop. It makes me sad to think that I won't be under the hood of a car anymore. I mean I love driving and racing but that shop gave me something when I had nothing. It's going to be hard to say goodbye. I send a quick text to Rob, my boss, letting him know I won't be in today and tell him I have big news. I know he'll be happy for me because that's the type of person he is but it still sucks to leave him behind. Rob took me under his wing when I was just sixteen years old. I was running with a questionable crowd and doing even more questionable things. Instead of doing what most people would have, he saved me. Leaving him is going to be a hard one.

I go to the door marked security and Patrick opens it up wide with a bright smile. "It's nice to see you again Miss Sutton."

"Thanks Patrick. It looks like you'll be seeing a lot of me. I'm officially the new Revv-It Racing driver." I smile at him. There's something about Patrick that reminds me of Rob.

He slaps his thigh. "Well, I'll be. That's the best news all day. Congratulations."

"Thank you. They sent me down to get a security badge made." I hand him the paperwork. He ushers me inside and gets my picture before uploading it and making the badge. For a man that's older he sure can use the electronics. Within fifteen minutes I have my badge and I'm ready to go. As I'm leaving out, I look over my shoulder at Patrick. "What's your favorite thing to eat?"

Patrick's smile goes large. "Apple pie and whipped cream."

I nod and head out the door. I'm admiring my badge when I nearly run into somebody. When I look up I see Maxton. "I'm sorry. I guess I was in dream land."

He chuckles. "Nothing wrong with that. No harm, no foul." His eyes move to my hands to take in the badge. "So, it's official, you're the new driver?"

"Yeah, seems like it." I shrug as unease comes over me.

Maxton nods his head. "That's good. You'll do great out there this season. This team needs a pick me up after the last couple of seasons."

I chuckle. "I don't know about that. Rathe's rookie season was pretty epic."

I watch as he gets a faraway look in his eyes. "Yeah, until that wreck. Damn, that messed the entire team up. Shook everyone to their core. Rathe is a damn good driver but he holds back now. I have a feeling you might give him a run for his money."

Shaking my head I laugh at that thought. "I don't know about that. I'm pretty sure he's not a fan of mine."

Rathe appears behind Maxton. His eyes narrow into a glare at me but not before I get to see those hypnotizing pools of chocolate. My heart skips a beat as the air shifts or maybe it's just me. At this point who knows? Rathe steps around Maxton and I. When he doesn't hear Maxton follow him, he asks, "Are you coming or what?"

Maxton gives me an apologetic smile. "I guess I'll be seeing you around."

"Yeah, I guess you will," I reply as he walks away. I turn around and watch them leave. I shouldn't because it's obvious that Rathe wants nothing to do with me but for some reason I can't shake him.

Eleven

Rathe

I'm lying in bed counting the rotations of the ceiling fan above me. My mind is trying to come up with a legit excuse to give to Tucker as to why I'm not showing up for test runs again today. It's been four technical work days since I've been to the track. I've given lame excuse after lame excuse as to why I can't be there. Tucker knows they're all a lie. Maxton knows it too. I'm killing time, licking the wounds that my ego received after getting slapped in the face with Sutton. I know that the team needs some wins and I know I didn't deliver last season but it still sucks to know that everyone else thinks you can't deliver either.

Sighing, I sit up on the side of my bed and run my hands through my hair. I need to get my shit together but how can you beat an invisible rival? I mean Sutton I can beat. I can climb into my car and race around that track, I can prove she's not the best. I can fight off the pull she has on me but I can't fight the invisible rival. I can't fight the anxiety, memories and all consuming panic that courses through my body. There's no cure for them. I can't outrun them. I'm just stuck.

I walk over to the floor to ceiling glass windows that line the back wall of the room, overlooking my backyard, pool and the beach just beyond that and pull the curtains back. The sun fills the room and I squint against the attack. I've learned this house like the back of my hand so luckily being temporarily blinded isn't that big of a deal. By the time I reach the hallway I'm good to go. I move around the house that I bought the day after I signed my contract with Revv-It. It's too large for just me but I was younger and cockier then. My plan was to show the world that I was going to own it. I wanted the biggest and best of everything. This house was just one of the many things on that list.

It wasn't until after the wreck when I got released from the hospital and walked into this large, empty house that I realized how dumb and naive I had been. I should sell this house and downsize but for some reason I can't let it go. Maybe, this is the last thing that I have to remind me of who I used to be. I'm scared to lose that version of me completely.

In the kitchen I start cooking eggs and bacon for a breakfast burrito when I hear the doorbell echo throughout the quiet space. Turning the burner all the way down to the lowest setting I head to the door. To say I'm surprised when I open the door would be an understatement. Tucker is standing there with his arms crossed over his broad chest, for an older man he's in relatively good shape. His eyes are hard and unforgiving and I know I'm on his shit list now. His mouth is frowning at me. "Well, it's good to see you're still alive considering all the excuses I've heard these past few days for why you aren't at the track."

I look away, guilt swims through my veins. I'm also not a good liar so I know I can't look in his eyes and tell him any of my excuses were true. "Yeah, I've just been under the weather."

Tucker scoffs and scoots past me to come into my house. "More like licking your bruised ego if you ask me."

I slam the door. Most people don't handle criticism well. Sadly, I'm one of them. My defenses go onto high alert. "Well, why don't you come on inside," I comment, my tone sarcastic.

"Looks like I'm already inside. I had to invite my own self in since you seemed to have lost all your damn manners. I mean I could have stood out there all damn morning if I hadn't barged right on in." Tucker challenges me but I just shake my head and walk away. I've got food cooking and this is a legit excuse right now. I hear his footsteps following behind me. "Well, you look fine."

Maybe, if I ignore him, he'll go away. However, he starts to whistle the theme song to the Brady Bunch and it gets on my nerves. I grind my teeth to keep from letting him know how irritating it is. Finally, on the fifth round of it I snap. "What the hell are you doing here Tucker?"

"Apparently, I need to drag my star driver to the track since he can't seem to find his way."

I roll my eyes. "I'm not your star driver anymore, you have Sutton for that." I sound like a spoiled, temperamental kid and the worst part is I know it but I can't seem to stop it. Ever since the first day I saw Sutton I haven't been able to shake her. Those brief moments I've been around her have done something to me. The moment I lay eyes on her my skin hums with anticipation. If she wasn't my biggest rival, I'd probably drop to one knee and ask her to marry me. But Sutton is my rival. She's the person who has now put my job in jeopardy and if I don't have this job then I don't even know who I am. I can't keep daydreaming about her. I have to beat her.

Tucker sighs. "Really Rathe?"

"What?" I bite out. My tone is harsh, too harsh for the guy that handed me this life.

"You're still my driver. Just because Sutton is there now doesn't mean that you aren't. It doesn't mean you get to skip out on test runs and what not. The team needed another driver. We went all last season to honor Chris' memory but this season has to be different. I need her and you. We need wins and sponsors to keep going, you know how this works." Tucker stares at me. I can feel him begging me to understand. That's the thing...I do understand. I understand all of it but I just don't want to admit it.

I toss my plate onto my counter with more force than I intended. The clatter echoes throughout the house. Both of my hands run through my hair before scrubbing at my face. "I don't know what to do Tucker." The silence hangs between us while he waits for me to process and say what I want. "Do you remember the night you approached me and offered me a test drive?"

He nods his head slowly. "I remember that like it was yesterday. This tall, lanky kid who drove the hell out of a car and managed to pull out a win in the last few seconds. It was one of those races that embeds into every membrane of your body. You and the other driver fought tooth and nail. You guys had us standing on our tip toes trying to see who was crossing that line first."

The question that I'm scared to know the answer to is on the tip of my tongue. "If I hadn't won that race...would you have approached me?"

"Yes," Tucker replies instantly. His voice is steady and firm. There isn't a single ounce of hesitation or disappointment there. "I didn't pick you because you won, Rathe. I picked you because you had that star quality about you. You drove that car with such ease. You became one with the car and the road and that's not something that is easy to do. It's not something anyone can teach, you have to be born with it." He stands up and walks around the counter until he's in my space. "You need to find that place within you again. You are too damn talented to be taken down by this. You've worked too hard. Fight whatever battle you need to and get back in this game. You and Sutton together, could change this whole damn season."

"What if I can't?" I whisper. Part of me hopes he doesn't even hear it but in true Tucker fashion he does.

He chuckles. "You can and you will. I know you Rathe. You just need to breathe and let go of it all. Leave it all behind, that season, the wreck, Chris. I know it's hard to do but the moment you slide behind the wheel of that car and pull onto that track you have to leave it behind if you want to move forward." I eventually nod my head so he knows that I hear him. Tucker's hand lands on my shoulder and squeezes it in reassurance. "Your ass better be at the track today. No more slacking, do you hear me?"

"Yes sir," I tell him.

He pats my back a couple of times before he leaves. I listen until I hear the door shut. My appetite is gone so I just head upstairs to shower and get dressed so I can get to the track. Tucker's words keep replaying in my mind. I have to leave it all behind to move forward.

Twelve

Sutton

It'd been days since I'd seen Rathe. Ever since the day I officially signed my contract he'd been missing. According to Maxton he was just under the weather but I couldn't help but feel like I was somehow to blame for it. I'm not trying to sound conceited. Maybe, it's just a coincidence but either way I was starting to doubt everything. It's like in Twilight when Edward goes missing and Bella can't help but feel responsible in some way. I'm Bella right now. Yes, I've seen Twilight. Secretly, I love it but I always blame it on Evanna because, let's face it, you just know by looking at her that she's going to be into sparkly vampires.

Since it's been days since Rathe last showed his face at the track you can imagine my surprise when I pull into the parking lot and see his truck parked there. My heart does a little flip flop which annoys me. I've stopped trying to figure out what is going on with my feelings for Rathe. It's too complicated and I don't do complicated plus, it's not like I even know the guy. He could have a girlfriend for all I know so I've given up trying to decipher why he makes my skin feel like I've touched electricity and my heart does flip flops. None of it matters anyways. I'm here to race...end of story.

I climb out of my car after parking and head to the gates. Patrick spots me and unlocks the gate before I ever even get my badge out. I smile at him and hold out a plastic bowl for him. "Apple pie again Miss Sutton?"

"Of course with ice cream. Hopefully, it didn't melt too badly on my way over," I tell him.

Patrick waves his hand dismissively. "It's ice cream, it doesn't need to be frozen to be good. I'll drink it if I have to," he admits with a chuckle.

I laugh as I picture that. "That's good to know. Well, I better get out to the track."

"Yeah, you've got some possible competition today."

Nodding my head I tell him, "I saw his truck in the parking lot but I never know what to expect from Rathe."

"None of us do but he's a good boy just having a rough go of things right now. You probably scare him a little because you're so good. It's hard for a man to admit a lady, especially a beautiful lady, is better at something than him." Patrick smiles one of the biggest smiles I've ever seen.

"Well, I don't know about all that but based on the smile on your face there's a story to be told and I definitely want to hear it later."

Patrick nods his head. "There's always a story Miss Sutton. You better get on in there but you be safe, you hear?"

"Yes sir," I tell him as I salute him. I step into the designated room I was given to change into my Revv-It racing suit that is required by Indy racing before heading out to the track. I'm finishing up the braid in my hair when I meet up with Tucker. "Good morning."

"Good morning Sutton. You'll have to wait a few minutes while Rathe finishes up his laps," Tucker explains.

I nod my head. "No problem. I'm glad to see he's back."

Tucker looks at me, he studies me for a moment before he finally says. "You really mean that, don't you?"

"Yeah, of course, why?" I can feel my eyebrows pull together in confusion.

He shakes his head. "Most drivers I've worked with or know wouldn't be excited to see their competition back on the track."

"Oh well, he seems like a good driver even if he is stuck inside his head too much right now. I'd love to race against him without all that and really see what he can do. Maybe, one day I can get that chance. Anyways, I'm all for the comeback story and I have a feeling that Rathe McCall is about to have one hell of a comeback story." I watch as he speeds around the track with ease. It reminds me that even though we're on the same team, he's my biggest competition. If he can stay out of his head, he's going to give me a run for my money.

"That he will. So, did you and Evanna find a place yet?" Tucker asks.

The smile that crosses my face is automatic. "Yes, it's awesome. Just signed off on it yesterday. It's a few blocks away from the beach and it's just perfect for the two of us."

"If you girls need any help moving things you just say the word. Most of the crew would be happy to help."

The offer makes my heart happy. I've never had anyone I could rely on except for Evanna but somehow it feels like I was meant to be a part of Revv-It Racing all along. "Thanks." I watch as Tucker's eyes switch back to the track, his body goes rigid and his jaw is obviously clenched. "Everything okay?"

He nods his head slowly. "Yeah, this is about the time where Rathe starts to flashback. I'm hoping today is better." I turn my head to the track and watch with Tucker to see what Rathe does. As he comes up to the turn he slows but he doesn't back down like the last time I watched him. The car stays at just the right angle and he makes it through. It's like the entire place releases the air they had been holding. He may have still let up on the gas but at least he didn't stop in the middle of the track like I had seen him do before, that's a huge improvement. For whatever reason the sense of happiness and pride comes over me for Rathe. Mentally, I kick myself because once again nothing makes sense.

****

My test run went really well. The car and I are getting used to one another. I'm learning the track and how to navigate the car with ease. It's difficult to be comfortable in a new car. As a driver you get adjusted to the way your car moves. You have to get in sync with it, find the rhythm and the comfort of it.

As I pull my car into the pit, I feel everything in me relax. That was my best test run I've had yet. I shaved five seconds off my time from yesterday. I couldn't be happier with that if I tried. I climb out of the car and pull my helmet off, the fresh air dances across my skin, cooling me off. That's the biggest difference between street racing and Indy racing, the required gear. The uniform we use is for good reason but it's hot as hell. I'm definitely not used to it. "Sutton, you did great! That was your best run yet," Tucker calls out to me as he approaches, clapping.

"Thanks Tuck! I can't believe I shaved that much off my previous time," I tell him as pride swells in my chest.

Tucker's smile is contagious. "I can. I knew you had it in you all along. So, tomorrow I'll need you here at ten sharp. We're having a meeting concerning the upcoming sponsors and appearances you'll need to be present for. It'll be you and Rathe mainly."

"Appearances?" I ask. I hadn't really considered that I would need to make appearances. I guess I should have realized that was part of the deal. Rathe is often in the spotlight at various charity functions and what not. I guess I just didn't add the two together.

Tucker nods his head. "Yeah, they'll give you the schedule. All you have to do is show up. Sometimes, they'll even send a car to pick you up. The schedule will cover all of that." I nod as Tucker walks away. I've never been a big people person. For the most part I've been a loner. Evanna was always the social butterfly. People don't take to me the way they do her. It's kind of like Katniss and Peeta from Hunger Games, another great reference thanks to Evanna. At the end of the day though, I'll never win people's favorite, my life has made me come across cold and hard. I'm not sure how I'm going to get through all of this junk to get to the driving.

Thirteen

Sutton

I'm lying on the couch in a sugar coma with Supernatural playing on our Netflix when Evanna shows up. She takes one look at me then the TV and she knows something is up. "Okay, talk to me?"

"There's nothing to talk about," I mumble as I stretch to see the screen around her.

Evanna scoffs. "Yeah right and I'm the queen of England. There is definitely something to talk about. You only binge watch Supernatural when you need a pick me up."

"That's not true," I tell her. I mean it totally is true but I'll deny it anyways. I've been in a funk since Tucker told me I had to do all this press stuff. I'm mentally kicking myself for not considering that sooner.

She gives me what I would call a mom look. You know the one where a mom looks at her child and then all of a sudden everything just comes flooding out of their mouths. Evanna has that look, I don't know how but she does. I've never seen it on anyone but her. I advert my eyes to keep from voicing my fears out loud. "Oh, don't you look away from me Sutton. You're going to tell me what the hell is going on."

I sigh, dramatically. "Nothing is going on except you are blocking my view of Jensen Ackels which could be dangerous for you."

Evanna grabs the remote before I can even register what she's doing. She cuts the TV off and then takes a seat on our now bare coffee table. Our apartment is packed into boxes that are stacked along the walls. Now, I'm worried that maybe we've jumped the gun. What if I can't pull off all this extra stuff that comes along with being an Indy racer car driver? "What's going on Sutton?"

I sit up. "I have to do a bunch of appearances apparently for Revv-It Racing."

"So?" Evanna says with a shrug, like it's no big deal. I guess I should have expected that reaction considering that she loves being the center of attention.

"So, that's a big deal. You know I don't do well with being the center of attention." I shrug and advert my eyes.

Evanna shakes her head. "That's not true you do just fine when you win a race and the crowd surrounds you."

I shake my head. "That's different. I did something to deserve that attention. I won the race."

"You've done something to deserve the attention now too. You've become the first female Indy race car driver on the Revv-It Racing Team. You are literally one in a million right now Sutton. Don't you see how many little girls you're going to inspire by doing this. You deserve this attention whether you see it or not." Evanna smiles at me and as her words start to sink in I feel my nerves calm down. "You feel better, don't you?"

"Yes, wise one," I tell her as I stick my tongue out at her. Evanna starts laughing and we spend the rest of the evening watching Supernatural and eating junk food, which is basically us every night. I wake up a few hours later to see Netflix has timed out and Evanna is asleep on the other side of the couch. I grab a blanket and cover her up before heading to my bedroom. As I lie in bed watching my ceiling fan make slow rotations the worry comes back. What if I'm not good enough to do this whole professional driver thing?

I get up and grab my laptop which thankfully I haven't packed yet and google Rathe McCall. Most of the videos and articles I find are either about his outstanding rookie year and the wreck that almost ended it or his extracurricular activities with the many models he's dated in the past. Finally, I stumble across what I was looking for. Rathe McCall and his time with the press. There's articles about functions he's appeared at and even some videos. I watch him as he works the crowd. His voice is deep and rich, impossible to ignore. His smile is wide and sincere and makes my toes curl. Everything about him is perfect in these videos. He says the right things, reacts at the right times. Rathe is a natural with the press and I envy him right now.

I study him trying to learn what I can from the man that clearly knows exactly what he's doing when he steps in front of the camera. He woos the crowd in the blink of an eye. I need to be able to do that. Rathe is so different in these videos though from the one I see at the track daily. This one is open and full of life with a smile that could make a blind person see again. The one on the track is sullen and withdrawn, lost in the darkness of his mind waiting for his demons to rear their ugly little heads. Maybe, we are both struggling more than we want to admit.

Fourteen

Rathe

My alarm goes off earlier than normal. At first, I have the urge to silence it, but then I remember I need to be at the track early today because we are going to get our press schedule. This was the part of being a professional driver that I had expected to hate my first year. However, I learned pretty quickly that it's not that bad. You just need to smile and nod at the right time. Memorize scripts with what to say and then say things at the right time. I learned to act like the camera was just another person that I'm talking to in the crowd. The moment you allow the camera to become something bigger it will own you. You have to play it off like it's no big deal.

Those words keep filling my mind all morning, no matter what I'm doing. Those were the words of advice that Chris gave me right before we walked on stage to announce some winner at some award show. I can't even remember the name or the award but I remember my hand shaking and my body being covered in sweat. I was a nervous wreck. I just knew I was going to lose my food at any moment and I was terrified it was going to be on the stage in front of the crowd and camera. It would haunt me for my entire career but then Chris came up. He took one look at me and laughed to himself mostly. He patted my back and told me to calm down then explained how he saw the camera when it was sitting in front of him. Ever since then I run those words through my head before any press situation, I have to be in.

Last year was rough, though. I was hearing his words but feeling his absence. From the moment I had signed that line on the Revv-It contract he had been by my side. We went to every race together, every event, every press junket. We showed our united front as teammates. Last year I was alone. The questions at the beginning of the season we're so hard. I couldn't run from them. I had to act as if I wasn't haunted by the memories of the wreck that took Chris' life on the track that day. I managed and to the world I seemed like I had everything together but in reality, I was falling apart.

This year, however, I will have Sutton by my side. The gorgeous girl who the camera will love. Nothing will phase her. With looks like hers I'm sure she is used to being the center of attention. Hell, she'll probably do anything to get it. It's obvious that she was made for the press, fame and limelight. Most drivers cringe at the idea of it. We just want to drive but we have to deal with all the other crap in order to get to the track but Sutton will be a pro at this.

I see her car sitting in the parking lot as I pull up to the race track. My mood instantly goes downhill even though I don't know why. I have no reason to dislike Sutton. She's done nothing to me really. It's just the idea of her, the threat of her that gets to me. I've never had to second guess myself once I was behind the wheel of a car but ever since that wreck it seems like that's all I do. I lost what Tucker used to call my natural ability. Sutton seems to have it though and that's what frustrates me. I should be on the top of the leaderboard. I should have had a winning season. She should be scared of me on the track but instead I see the little flashes of pity in her eyes when she looks at me and it pisses me off.

As I reach the gate Patrick waves at me. I give him the best smile I can muster and wave. "Good morning Patrick, how are you doing today?" I ask.

"Real good Mr. McCall. How are you?"

I shake my head. Patrick is like that grandfather that you never had. "Patrick, I've told you how many times to call me Rathe, please and I'm well, thank you for asking." He nods his head at my request yet I know tomorrow as I approach, he'll once again refer to me as Mr. McCall and it drives me crazy. As I look through the glass windows he sits behind I notice a large piece of apple pie. "I didn't know you liked apple pie."

Patrick smiles and nods his head. "Yes sir, it's my favorite. Miss Sutton brings me a piece almost every day."

That really shouldn't rub me the wrong way but it does. It's ridiculous. "Well, my mom makes the best apple pie in the world. Next time she makes some I'll grab you some slices."

"That's not necessary Mr. McCall," Patrick tells me. I give him a stern look and he chuckles. "Rathe."

I laugh. "Well, if apple is your favorite then it's totally necessary." Patrick finally nods. "Well, I better get in there. We get to find out our press schedules today."

"Least favorite part of the job?"

"Always has been, always will be but it comes with the territory so I have to embrace it to some extent. You have a good day Patrick," I tell him as I wave goodbye to him.

Patrick smiles and waves back. "You too Rathe."

The elevator music plays soft and low as I ride up to the next floor of the building. Considering how much I dislike elevators I should have just taken the stairs but knowing that Sutton is already here makes me feel like I'm running late. I'm not but I feel it. As I exit the elevator I'm greeted by a few employees. I don't remember their names from the brief time I've met them but I say hello. When I reach the all glass conference room I see Mr. Wilson, Tucker and Sutton sitting around the table laughing.

I take a deep breath and attempt to remind myself that Sutton is my teammate and I have no reason to dislike her.

As I enter all three sets of eyes turn to find me. "Good morning Rathe," Mr. Wilson calls out to me.

"Good morning Mr. Wilson. Tucker, Sutton," I tell them with a nod of my head as I move towards a seat across from them where a stack of papers is lying in front of. "How is everyone?"

"We're well and early apparently. Since everyone is here should we go ahead and start?" Mr. Wilson asks no one in particular. We nod and then he opens his packet of paperwork. I do the same and I notice a lot of the same press stuff from the last couple of seasons along with a few new ones. I chance a glance at Sutton and see that her blue gray eyes are wide and wild. She looks like a baby deer in headlights. Part of me feels for her because I remember the first time, I saw this packet. My look was probably similar to that. Chris' words float back into my mind but I don't say anything. Over the next hour we go over our schedule. Between press, charity functions, sponsor events and races, Sutton and I are going to be incredibly busy.

As soon as Mr. Wilson dismisses us Sutton jumps up. I shouldn't take notice of how her jeans mold to her every curve. Or how her worn band t-shirt looks like perfection on her without making her look like she doesn't care. Her long chocolate brown hair is down and curled today. The shine of it glistens under the lights above. It looks so soft and a part of me itches to reach out and run my fingers through her hair just to see if it's as soft as it looks. I watch as she rushes from the conference room. My blood pumps in overtime and I have to fight my overactive imagination before I get carried away.

Sutton seemed worried and it keeps hanging around in the back of my mind, making me feel bad for her but really, she has nothing to worry about. She'll be a natural. I'm the one who has to worry about her taking my spot. It's at this moment that I decide I'm going to have to practice double time to get back to where I was if I want to stay on top.

Fifteen

Sutton

I moved so quickly that I'm dizzy as hell now or maybe it's because this schedule in my hands feels like the weight of the world. Either way if I make it out to the elevator, I'll be lucky. I step slowly and try to take in tiny breaths through my mouth. I remember reading somewhere that helps nausea which I'm starting to feel thanks to the constant spinning of the room. I was never one of those kids who was a fan of merry-go-rounds or roller coasters. I love fast cars but everything else I like at a nice and normal speed. I'm so zoned out that I don't even hear him approach from behind me until I smell his woodsy cologne. It should be an annoying scent. I mean who smells like the woods in the middle of the damn city but on Rathe, well, let's face it the scent is kind of intoxicating.

"Well, I think you might have high tailed it out of that conference room faster than you race around that track." I don't respond. I think I'm in shock with my building anxiety. "What, cat's got your tongue?" I can hear the irritation lurking in his tone. He's trying to get a reaction out of me and I'm not giving it to him. His smirk is in place, eyes guarded when I turn my head to look up at him. I don't know what he sees. I can only imagine what a mess I am right now but whatever he's seeing causes his facade to falter. "Hey...are you alright?" I just nod my head, numbly. My tongue feels like cotton in my mouth and there's a lump in my throat I can barely breathe around, let alone talk with. His eyes swim with worry. "Sutton, you need to speak." He reaches out, his large hands grip my biceps, trying to pull me back into the now but I'm not sure I can find it. "Do I need to call for help?" his voice shows a hint of panic and I manage to shake my head no. His face shows a bit of relief. "Can you tell me what's wrong?" I open my mouth but it's just too dry to speak so I end up closing it again. "Okay, come on chatterbox." Rathe pulls me into the elevator and we head back down. The ride down only takes a couple of seconds really but it feels like hours in the tight space. When the doors open Rathe grabs my hand and pulls me down the hallway before taking the left and heading down to his room. I'm sure there's a better term for this area but I haven't learned it yet. Basically, it's like a dressing room for us, we each have one and each is filled with certain things we like to have on hand. Rathe unlocks his door and ushers me inside.

I try to take it in because it's so different from mine. The walls are painted a beautiful and soothing ocean blue color. The furniture is dark gray and oversized. The kind of furniture that you know you'll just sink down into the moment your bum hits the seat. Suddenly, I feel incredibly tired. As if he can read my mind, Rathe leads me over to the couch and nudges my shoulders with his hands until I sit down. There's a large TV mounted onto the wall in front of me with a huge stereo system underneath that. There's a guitar in the corner of the room, sitting on the stand. It's beautiful but something that's definitely been used before. I watch as he opens the minifridge and pulls a bottle of water from it before he crosses the room and hands it to me. I take it, thankful for the moisture and as soon as it hits my tongue it feels like all my prayers have been answered.

"Thanks," I mumble quietly. My throat is still scratchy.

Rathe smirks. "She does speak!"

I glare at him which causes him to chuckle which then leads my toes to attempt to curl inside their Converse. It's ridiculous but this man causes some strange reactions within me. "I speak just fine."

"I beg to differ darlin'. I mean you couldn't say a damn word a few minutes ago upstairs but who knows maybe that's just the effect I have on you," he tells me with a wink.

I scoff. "As if."

"You sound so Clueless when you say that."

My eyes narrow once more. "You've watched Clueless?" I somehow cannot picture that. It just doesn't seem like Rathe, not that I really know him.

He nods his head as he takes a seat in the chair that is still too close to me yet too far away. "I do have a sister."

"Bless her heart," I tell him using my best southern accent.

Now, he scoffs. "You should be blessing my heart. She's the devil sometimes."

"I'm sure she had to be with you around. You do have this charming effect on people, like bringing out the worst in them."

"Ouch, your words wound me Sutton." He grabs at his heart as if I actually hurt him.

I shrug. "The truth hurts. Maybe, you should work on that."

"Noted." We sit in silence, both of us staring at the other, daring one another to make the next move. Now, that my mind and heart are moving normally again, this moment feels so strange. "So, now do you want to tell me what the hell that was upstairs? I mean since you like to be so truthful."

I shrug and look away. "The schedule overwhelmed me, that's all."

Rathe chuckles and it causes two reactions. First of all it's irritating and second, it calms the nerves dancing within my body. "I thought girls like you would live for the spotlight, so what's the issue?"

"Girls like me?" My voice rises at his accusation.

One of his large hands comes up to scratch at his beard. "Yeah, girls like you. You know the hot, high maintenance, rich girls. The ones who've had everything handed to them on a silver platter with their trust fund waiting as soon as they blow out the candles on their eighteenth birthday cake."

I'm pretty sure my mouth is on the floor now. He can't be serious. There's no way he actually thinks I'm anything like the girls he just described. I always envied those girls but I was definitely not one of them. "You're kidding right?"

He shakes his head. "Nope."

"You're an ass. One thing...you don't know me," I tell him as I stand up and make my way to the door.

His laughter causes me to stop. "Oh, but I do. I think I know you better than you think."

The confidence in his words fuels my anger. I look over my shoulder at him. "I can promise you that you don't. You don't know the first thing about me and never will." I yank the door open and step into the hallway where the cool air rushes past me. I didn't realize how hot it had been inside his room. My anger isn't helping things. There's only one thing that will for sure calm me down now. I need to race.

Sixteen

Sutton

I'm sitting on my bed, sipping a soda, replaying the day when I hear the front door open. Today was a fail in every way. After getting our press schedule and my run in with Rathe McCall, I was a mess on the track. I clocked my worst time ever. I just couldn't keep my head in the game no matter how hard I tried. Eventually, Tucker called me in and insisted I call it a day. I did but I couldn't help feeling like a failure. Evanna appears in the doorway, her sky-high heels in her hands, "What's up bestie?"

I sigh and flop back to lay on my bed. The mattress moves as she lies down beside me. "I got the press schedule today which is so much worse than I thought it would be. I kind of had a panic attack that Rathe had to save me from but then he went on to tell me exactly how he feels about me."

Evanna lets out a low whistle. "So, is that a good thing?"

I shake my head. "Nope, not unless you think someone believing you are a privileged spoiled attention whore is a good thing."

She sits up abruptly then turns around to face me. "He said that?" Her voice rises with her anger.

I shrug, playing it off like it's no big deal. "Yeah, he clearly thinks he knows me without actually knowing me."

"Please, tell me you corrected him," Evanna says.

"No, I mean what's the point. I mean he may be my teammate technically and once upon a time a fantastic driver but he's clearly judgmental. He's made up his mind about me as is so why bother?"

Evanna's eyes bug out. "Because he's wrong!"

"Yes, he is but I could talk until I'm blue in the face and it won't change his opinion. The best thing I can do is just concentrate on this upcoming press tour and racing. That's what I'm getting paid for." I pull my bottom lip between my teeth because I really just want to end this conversation but I know better than to try and change it. Evanna will only push it more if I do.

Evanna stands up. "You know what? You're right! So, we're going to practice as much press stuff as we can. I'll videotape you, ask questions, help you memorize scripts, whatever you need. You're going to rock this press tour and win these races and leave Rathe McCall in the damn dust."

Fierce Evanna is kind of a scary Evanna. I haven't seen her this determined in a long time. "Easy there."

She shakes her head. "Rathe just made himself two badass rivals. I hope he can handle it."

****

Over the next couple of days Evanna and I practice everything possible in our free time. She has filmed so much that I actually feel strange when the camera isn't shoved in my face. We got the first script for the tire launch party. The first stop in the press tour is Detroit, Michigan. Our new tire sponsor for the upcoming season, Burnout Tires. I already have the entire script memorized. The problem is I sound like a robot when I deliver it. Evanna keeps giving me pointers like loosen up or laugh here but it's just not me. I'm not sure how I'm going to manage to get through this.

I'm just slipping my hair through my ball cap when there's a knock on the door. I open it and to my surprise I see most of the pit crew from Revv-It. Tucker is in the front of the group. "It's moving day, right?"

I'm stunned speechless but Evanna pops up behind me. "It sure is and you guys are lifesavers. I mean seriously. Sutton and I would be at this for days if we had to move everything ourselves. Come on in," she ushers them inside. "Luckily, it's the boxes that have to go and the electronics. We're leaving the furniture since it's all seen better days anyways. I will spring for pizza and wings once we are finished."

Tucker waves his hand dismissively. "That's not necessary. This is just how it is to be part of the Revv-It Racing Team. We take care of our own."

I'm scanning the guys as Evanna and Tucker talk but then something shocking happens. Rathe McCall appears in my doorway with a beautiful raven haired girl. Rathe moves his sunglasses to the rest in the collar of his navy blue t-shirt. My blood boils both with anger for his assumptions and want for him. It's so confusing. "Well, since my brother has seemed to have lost all his manners allow me to introduce myself." The girl steps forward and extends her hand, her honey eyes are kind. "I'm Ryann McCall, Rathe's sister, the better half. You must be Sutton."

I smile and take her hand. "Yes, I am. It's nice to meet you."

"You too! I had to come and help out and meet the girl that has my brother so riled up," Ryann says with a laugh.

"Ryann," Rathe calls out like she's a child in trouble.

I have to bite back the chuckle threatening to bubble out. "Well, as you can see, he's starting to get defensive. You know how men are."

"All too well," I tell her.

"Let's get this stuff moved and we can gossip about my brother some more," Ryann says as she links her arm through mine.

Everything is moved and sitting inside of our new house on a side of town I never thought I would call home. This part of town was one of those places that when I drove through, I yearned for more. In my mind I was never good enough to live here and it still seems like there might be some kind of mistake. It seems like a dream come true in so many ways. "So, I'm trying to figure something out."

His voice comes from behind me. It's low enough that I know he has to be just a couple feet away. I turn around and find him studying me. "Well, I'd advise you not to try and figure things out. You might hurt that small minded brain of yours."

"Ouch, coming with the punches right out of the gate I see," Rathe says as he steps closer to me.

I shrug. "I was never one to beat around the bush."

"Guess that makes two of us," Rathe replies. Silence falls between us, both of us daring the other to speak next in this unknown challenge we've placed ourselves in.

"Why are you even here?" I finally ask.

He shrugs and looks away. "Curiosity killed the cat right?" My eyebrows pull together in confusion. Rathe sighs. "Technically we're teammates and Revv-It is big on making sure you help each other out."

Now, he's just being weird and confusing. "I'm lost. What does that have to do with curiosity"

"I wanted to see where you were moving to. I got to admit though, this isn't that impressive. I mean I figured we'd be moving your stuff into a mansion or something." Rathe crosses his arms over his well-defined chest and I watch as the sleeves of his shirt stretch against his muscles. I study the house behind him. The light seafoam green siding and white shutters called to both Evanna and I when we saw it. It felt fresh and airy. The white wrap around porch seemed like the perfect place for me to relax after a long day on the track and the backyard was large with enough trees to give shade if we ever decided to get a dog.

"Mansions aren't really my thing," I finally respond.

Rathe chuckles and I swear the sound dances across my skin. "What? Growing up in one was too much for you? Was that why you were living in that ratty apartment?"

Just like that he ruins the moment. His assumptions drive my anger back up full force. My jaw clenches and my eyes narrow into a glare. "Again, you don't know the first thing about me. Maybe, you should stop assuming you know everything about everyone. I'm sure you've heard the saying 'No one likes a know-it-all.' You should really consider that."

Rathe leans in towards me, his scent invades my senses. My nose takes a deep breath without my knowledge. That damn woodsy scent again. The scent that is going to haunt my dreams now. "Well, then I guess it's a damn shame that I know everything but then again I don't give a damn who likes me."

"Obviously but maybe instead of being concerned about who likes or what you think you know...you should concentrate on driving...and I don't know, winning a race or two this season," I bite out before I can shut my mouth. Rathe steps back so quickly you think I would have slapped him. I guess I kind of did, verbally anyways. For a moment I feel ashamed for the low blow but then I remember all of his assumptions about me. I step around and leave Rathe standing, looking stunned in my backyard.

Seventeen

Rathe

Wow, that's all I can think right now. Sutton could have kicked her leg out and kicked me where the sun don't shine and it would have hurt less than her parting words. I wasn't expecting her to lash out at me. I'm not saying I didn't deserve it because, let's face it, I've been nothing but an ass to her since the moment I met her but I didn't expect it. I'm at a loss of what to do right now. I've never wanted someone so badly in my life but at the same time I want her out of my life. I want to be the one on the track winning races for my team. She's that constant reminder of last season and the fact of how miserably I failed. Sutton is the face that will haunt my dreams because she's going to take them from me. I scrub a hand down my face. Slipping on my sunglasses I turn around and head back inside.

The moment I enter I hear Ryann laughing. I find her with Sutton and Evanna. That shouldn't upset me but it does. My jaw clenches and I bark out, "Come on Ryann. We're leaving!"

"Dude, what stick got up your ass?" Ryann asks as she stands up.

I walk past her without another word. She'll either follow or she won't. I don't have to worry about her because Maxton is here somewhere and if Ryann doesn't come with me, Max will make sure she gets home. However, I hear her footsteps behind me. I unlock the Range Rover and climb inside. Ryann does the same. She sits there with her arms crossed over her chest and anger simmering in her features. "Buckle up so we can go."

"I was having a conversation in case you failed to notice that."

I nod my head slowly. "Then by all means go finish it. Max can give you a ride home. Either way I'm leaving now."

"What the hell is wrong with you Rathe? I try to understand where you're coming from, what you're going through. Obviously, I can't. I never understood your need to race to begin with. I've never had to almost lose my life doing something I loved. I've never had to witness death like you did on the track that day..."

"Ryann..." I say as a warning.

She shakes her head. "No, you need to hear this. No one wants to tell you. They want to give you time to mourn or move past it but you aren't doing that. You're stuck in it. You relive it every day because you won't let it go."

"You don't know what the hell you're talking about," I bite out, barely able to control my temper.

Ryann scoffs. "Yes I do. Max, our parents and I all know. Tucker knows. The team knows Rathe. You haven't won a race since the wreck. Every time you back off and then blame it on the car but it's not your car, it's you. Now, you're mad because Sutton has showed up and she's great at what she does. Just as good as you but instead of being happy for her and embracing some friendly competition and the fact that she could help the team, you're rude to her. You're downright nasty to her. You've made all these assumptions about her but I'm pretty damn sure you're wrong."

"How would you know what I think about her?"

"I heard from Maxton what you've been saying about her. I don't think she's some rich bitch like you're assuming she is. You might want to actually take the time and get to know her."

"Are you done?" I ask her. I don't want to listen to my sister lecture me. I'm not in the mood. I find it really annoying and it's not even because of the lecture. It's just because she's right and I don't want to admit it out loud.

"No, not even close. I'll keep lecturing you until you get it through that stubborn head of yours. Look I'm sure she has a lot of assumptions about you too that are wrong but she hasn't really got to meet you. You've got this guard up with her and it's ridiculous," Ryann goes on. "She isn't here to hurt you or ruin your career."

I spin around and glare at her. "Really? Is that what you think?"

Ryann smirks. "Yes, it is."

"Then get the hell out of my vehicle," I tell her through clenched teeth.

She shakes her head. "She doesn't need to ruin your career or even relationships with other people, you're doing a great job of that all on your own big brother." Ryann opens the door and steps out. The door slams with an outstanding thud. I sit in my SUV along the sidewalk for a long time just trying to remember how to breathe.

As I pull onto the street, I know there's only one place I'll be able to decompress. I turn my Range Rover in the direction of the track. I don't know why I want to go to the one place that seems to cause me the most turmoil in my life right now but it's the only place I've ever felt like home. I need to find the person I used to be. I need to find the guy that found the track as comforting as his home, sometimes even more so. The man I used to be yearned to be on the asphalt, flying around like I had nothing to lose at top speeds. Nothing scared me more than the idea of not racing. I wish I knew where he went.

I've been sitting in the stands staring at the dark track in the distance when I hear the light footsteps. It's probably Max or

Ryann, possibly even Tucker but when I turn around the last person I expect to see is standing there. She looks no different than earlier aside from the fact that her hair is piled on top of her head in a messy bun and her face is clean of all makeup. She's freaking gorgeous, so much it almost hurts to look at her. The craziest thing is…I don't think she even realizes it. Sutton Pierce isn't just my rival, she's going to be my undoing.

"What are you doing here?" I ask her. My voice comes out harsher than I intended it to.

Sutton doesn't even flinch. Either she's got a really tough skin and she's used to the harshness of a tone or she's just got used to me being an ass to her. She looks out over the track and I watch her shoulders rise as she takes in a deep breath. "Sometimes I just need to be away from everyone. I just need the quiet and there's no place that silences my mind better than some asphalt."

I feel her words down the core of me. "I get that."

After a few moments of silence Sutton finally asks the loaded question I was waiting for, "What are you doing here?"

"My sister not so kindly told me what an ass I've been lately to just about everyone, but you especially. I just needed a place to think and try to find who I used to be again. "I hang my head because after Ryann's verbal lashing, I feel even worse about how I've treated Sutton since I've met her.

"Well, I won't argue with you there," she tells me as she moves forward, away from me. I should let her go. She clearly needs space and quiet to think about something but for some reason I get up and move towards her.

As I come up behind her I quietly tell her, "I'm sorry."

Sutton shrugs like it's no big deal. "Shit happens. Trust me I'm not losing sleep over your assy ways."

I chuckle. "That's good. I wouldn't want you to lose any beauty sleep, princess."

She scoffs. "You may need beauty sleep but some of us are naturally beautiful."

"Do you always bite back twice as hard?"

Sutton turns to look at me and smirks. "Oh honey, that's not my bite. That's just a nibble."

Damn, this girl is some form of a dream come true and I really don't think she sees it. "Then help the person that gets the bite."

"Amen!" Sutton laughs and it fills the silent night.

We stand side by side, both staring at the dark track. I'm beginning to think we're more alike than we originally thought. "Sutton?" She turns around to face me and I can see the question lurking in her blue eyes. "Can we start over?"

Uncertainty clouds her features and I wouldn't blame her if she told me no right now. Everyone, including myself, knows I deserve a big, fat, hell no from her but eventually Sutton smiles, it's a small smile but I'll take what I can get. She nods her head. "I'd like that."

"Me too but you're still my rival when we hit the track," I tell her.

"Damn right although try not to choke on my dust," she teases me with a wink. I laugh and she does too. A weight lifts off my shoulders and for the first time in months I feel like maybe the darkness isn't so dark after all.

Eighteen

Sutton

I'm finally starting to adjust to the new house. The first few nights I couldn't sleep for crap. I tossed and turned. The new bed and room just threw me off. Last night was the first night I actually slept and this morning I'm feeling great. I'm ready to hit the track and own it. However, that thought dies the moment I see Rathe's car slowing down as he comes into the second curve. I hold my breath and wait to see if he can manage to pull himself out of his head but it never happens. Eventually, the car just comes to a stop.

An idea pops into my head as I stare at his stalled car. I jog over to the pit crew and find Maxton. This idea is either total genius or crazy, I'm not sure which. "Max!"

He looks down at me from where he's sitting above the track. "Hey Sutton!"

"I have an idea...to help Rathe," I admit. Saying that out loud feels weird as hell. Max's eyes go wide. "Yeah, yeah, I know, crazy right?"

Maxton climbs down and joins me on the ground. "I'm not sure I heard you right up there, you said you had an idea to help Rathe?" I nod my head. "But why?"

"Rathe is a great driver and he needs to get back there. He needs help to find that version of himself again and I think I might have an idea. I don't know if he'll go for it or not though." Maxton's expression changes as he studies me and finally he agrees to hear my plan out. I tell him my idea and he agrees to it. I'm in my suit and car in record time. Tucker climbs the steps to sit above the track with Maxton as I pull out of the pit. I slow as I come up next to Rathe's car. He looks over at me, confusion is clear in his eyes. He pulls his helmet off and I do the same.

"What are you doing?" he asks.

"What does it look like I'm doing?" I counter back at him.

Rathe narrows his eyes at me. "It looks like you're on the track during my practice time, care to tell me why?"

"Last night you seemed to be searching for a different version of you. The version of you that owned this track. My guess is that you were much more competitive back then, am I right?" I ask him. He nods his head yes but I can tell that he still doesn't trust my reasoning. "You need some friendly competition to awaken that side of you again. So, I was thinking you and I could race a few laps."

"I don't know..." The hesitation in his voice pulls at my heart. I hate to see anyone struggle especially when it's something that they love as much as Rathe loves racing.

"Look, it's just you and me. We can start out slow and then speed up as you like. The risk is minimal with just the two of us on the track, less worry and anxiety," I add, trying to ease him into the idea. I don't want him to think I'm trying to say he's incapable of doing his job because I know he's not but it seems like he has a mental block when he races now and it's holding him back.

Rathe is quiet for a moment, he stares ahead at the track in front of him. He watches it as if it's going to magically give him an answer and I watch him, waiting for his answer. Finally, he turns back to me. "Why are you trying to help me?"

"That seems to be the most popular question of the day." I take a deep breath and look away, trying to give him an answer is easier said than done. I may be a girl but I don't do the mushy, talk your feelings out type of situations. That's Evanna's territory, not mine. I return my eyes back to his. "We started over, right?"

"Yeah."

"Then do I really need a reason aside from that?" I ask.

He nods his head. "You don't have to have one I guess but I think you do."

"Fine, if I know you are on the top of your game it's a challenge for me and I like a challenge. I like to push my limits on when I race. It's what I want." I give him an *'are you satisfied'* look.

Rathe shakes his head. "The moment you're on this track you'll have plenty of challenges. You'll have a handful of the best drivers Indy racing has ever seen. You don't need me to be on my top game to have a challenge."

Technically, he's right but it's not like I can admit that I feel some strange pull towards him. I can't even explain that to myself so telling him is out of the question so I go with the lame cop out answer. "You're my teammate and it's better for Revv-It if you're on top of your game. It'll be better for me because it's just one more challenge on the track. It all plays in together plus let's face it you were a fantastic driver. If I'm going to race against you, I want it to be against that version of you." Silence falls between us. We both hold each other's eyes until I finally ask, "So, what's it going to be?"

Rathe nods his head, his eyes determined. "Let's do it." We slip our helmets back on and nod at one another. We start from the second curve, the one that always seems to cause Rathe to back off. We aren't very fast at first and we do a couple of slower laps. I glance over and see Rathe give me a thumbs up. I'm assuming that means he wants to speed up so I'm not surprised that we both do. With each lap we accelerate a little more but so far Rathe hasn't backed off when we come up to the second curve. I'm excited for him.

We've hit a true racing speed and we're coming up to the second curve. I hold my breath as we come into the curve. If he's going to back off, now will be the time. I ease off just a little and watch his tires to see if he's going to let up. I'm sure everyone watching the two of us is holding their breath. I relax my grip as Rathe hits the straightaway without a moment of hesitation. Rathe pulls away from me and speeds up even more. There's a sense of pride that comes over me as I watch him speed away and towards the finish line. He may technically be my rival but I'm still happy for him. Now, if only he can do this in a real race situation.

Nineteen

Rathe

As I cross the finish line, ahead of Sutton and at a speed that I can be proud of I feel a weight lift off my shoulders. It's been so long since I've crossed this finish line with a time that makes me feel like myself that I'm not even sure how to process it. I come to a stop in the middle of the track and start to climb out of the car. Sutton comes up behind me and does the same. I reach for her hand once she's free of the seat belts and pull her out of the car and into my arms. Her scent engulfs me. She smells sweet, too sweet to be on this track or in my arms but she is. She squeals in shock as I spin her around. We both laugh and for the first time since the day of that wreck I feel like myself again...finally.

"You did it!" Sutton exclaims as I place her feet back on the ground.

I nod. "With a lot of help from you." I may hate to admit that to some extent but it's still the truth. I don't think I could have done what I just did if it wasn't for her help. She's like part the devil and part an angel. She's my rival and my cheerleader it seems.

"All I did was make a suggestion; it was up to you to take it. I'm so happy for you. How does it feel?" she asks. I don't get to answer her question because a crowd quickly builds around us, demanding our attention and pulling us in different directions. The pit crews, Maxton and Tucker are all there, cheering for me. It makes me feel like I'm on top of the world.

A few hours later and a lot more trips around the track, mostly by myself since they pulled Sutton out to have her fitted for outfits for the upcoming press stuff. I'm standing in my dressing room, staring at my reflection in the mirror. There's a light in my eyes that I haven't seen in a long time. My smile isn't forced for the first time in months. I look like the old me. I turn off the lights and step out of the room. As I turn to head for the hallway that will lead to the parking lot I bump into someone. "Shit! I'm sorry," I say as I look down to see who I just nearly ran over. To my surprise Sutton's blue gray eyes lock with mine.

She laughs. "It's okay. I wasn't looking either so no need to apologize."

"I didn't get a chance to actually thank you for today. We kind of got pulled in different directions before I could," I tell her.

I watch as a blush creeps up her skin and into her cheeks. She bites down on her lower lip, uncertainty colors her features. "I really didn't do anything. You don't need to thank me. The driving was all you. I'm glad the idea seems to have helped."

"It did. I haven't felt this good in months. It's like crossing that finish line at a top speed even though it wasn't an actual race set something free in me. It's like the old me raced back up within me," I tell her. She gives me a curious look and I shake my head. "I'm probably not making any sense."

Sutton giggles. "You kind of are. I mean not completely but enough that I get what you're attempting to say."

"Good." Silence falls between us and before I have time to have a second thought about it I ask, "Do you want to go grab some food and maybe a drink?"

Her eyes go wide. Clearly, she's shocked and if I'm being honest so am I. I didn't expect to ask her to hang out with me. I mean regardless of what happened today on the track Sutton is still technically my rival. Despite that though she just possibly saved my career and I can't help but feel grateful to her for that. It's all so confusing. I shouldn't want to spend time with her but

I do. She's gorgeous, smart, a hell of a driver and apparently forgiving if she could find it in herself to help me after how I've treated her. "Sure," she finally replies quietly after some hesitation.

When we get to the parking lot I offer to drive us and then bring her back to her car but she declines. So, we drive in separate cars to this little dive bar with the best food. It's a little hidden gem of the town. Only the townies know about this place. It's possible Sutton knows about it but since I'm not sure how long she's actually lived here I can't be sure. I pull around back and wait to see her headlights as she rounds the corner. She pulls in next to my SUV. As we meet in front of my vehicle I ask, "Have you ever been to Pat's?"

She shakes her head. "No, but I've heard of it. It supposedly serves the best hamburger and fries in town."

"Then you've heard right." We head inside. Benny, Pat's husband, is behind the counter filling a mug of beer from the tap as we enter. He waves a greeting, telling us to have a seat and he'll be right over.

As Sutton and I take a seat near the back of the dimly lit, smoke filled bar I take a moment to truly see her. She has an incredible strength and confidence in her movements but there's an underlying insecurity there too. I can tell by the way she fidgets when she thinks no one is looking. It makes me curious. It makes me want to know more about her. Benny heads over and takes our order. Sutton seems to relax into her chair a bit more and it makes me wonder if I have her pegged wrong. There's no way a rich princess type would be okay with a place like this, let alone heard about it. Pat's isn't exactly a place on the charts in that part of the world. Maybe, Ryann was right and I have everything all wrong but judging by the wall that seems to surround Sutton, I don't have a chance of finding out the truth. At least not tonight.

"You know it's rude to stare." Sutton raises her head from her phone and I've been caught red handed. I was definitely staring at her but I won't apologize.

I smirk. "Yeah, well sometimes you can't help but stare."

Sutton scoffs and shakes her head. "Oh really?" I nod my head in agreement. "And why is that Romeo?"

I shrug. "I don't like to deny myself the few things created of natural beauty in this world. I mean look around, it's easy to find something that's been made to be beautiful but it's difficult to find something or someone who has it naturally. You, Sutton Pierce, have that breathtaking natural beauty."

Her mouth is a slim, straight line, her eyes narrow as she studies me. Then she busts out laughing. It's loud and beautiful and hits me full in my gut. "That's a line of shit if I've ever heard one. Does that actually work on women?"

Just like that we're back on an even playing field. "You'd be surprised."

"By the lack of creativity on your part or lack of intelligence on their part?" She smirks and raises an eyebrow in question and I'll be damned if it's not the hottest things I've ever seen.

"Both darlin'," I tell her. She shakes her head and rolls her eyes. This girl is going to have me racing around more than just a track.

Twenty

Sutton

I'm stuffed with food. As much as I hate to admit it, Rathe was right, this food was amazing. I mean talk about melt in your mouth cheeseburger. I could live off these without a second thought. I'm also a little tipsy at this point. The more I drink, the better looking Rathe becomes which is hard to believe because he's already got that tall, dark and handsome thing going for him anyways. My stomach feels the flutter every time our eyes meet over the table. I'm acting like some high school girl with a crush but I don't know what else to do. Rathe causes some unusual reactions out of me for whatever reason.

Another drink is sitting in front of me. I take a sip before a song that I have never been able to ignore comes blaring through the bar. I Love Rock n' Roll by Joan Jett is playing which means I'm dancing, even if I look silly doing it. I jump up from my seat only to stumble into the table next to ours. Thankfully, it's empty but Rathe has some lighting fast reflexes because he's also out of his seat, his large strong hands locked around my elbows to steady me. His voice is deep and there's a slight hint of amusement in it. "Whoa there, where do you think you're going?"

I smirk up at him. "This is not a song to ignore. I'm going to dance. The question is...are you coming with me?"

Rathe chuckles and shakes his head. "Not a chance in hell darlin'. I don't dance."

"Well, that's a damn shame. I guess you'll be watching me then." I turn away from him and strut, more than necessary, towards the dance floor. I feel his eyes on my hips as they sway from side to side. My skin flushes from the heat of it. The moment that I hit the dance floor, the music and rhythm hits me and Rathe is forgotten as I begin to move to the music and sing along. The song is about halfway through when I let my faux leather moto jacket fall from my shoulders, onto the floor. Under the lights on the dancefloor I'm hot or maybe it's just all the movement. Either way the jacket needs to go for now.

I feel his presence near before I even turn around to see him standing just a few feet away with a wicked smile on his face, his eyes darkened with lust and my jacket laying over his arm. I make my way back towards him. "You're so much trouble Sutton."

I toss my hair to the side and smile at him sweetly. "I have no idea what you mean."

Rathe pulls his bottom lip between his teeth and leans forward. I can smell the small hint of whiskey on his breath and the warmth of his body sends shivers down my spine. My stomach flutters again. "I think you know exactly what I mean. You're putting on a show for me, not that I'm complaining."

"Who said the show was for you?" I make a spectacle of looking around the bar at the others sitting around. "I could be showing off for any of them." Rathe's eyes narrow and for a moment I think he's upset but he wraps his arms around my waist and yanks me into his body so quickly my head spins. The song has changed to some slow country song. Rathe moves us to the beat and I find it easy to follow him. "I thought you didn't dance."

He shrugs. "I can make an exception every now and then. Besides, I may have wanted an excuse to hold you."

I laugh. "Sure you did. You hate me so why would you want to hold me?"

"I don't hate you Sutton." His eyes seem serious but maybe that's just the alcohol in my veins making me think that.

"You're so confusing," I tell him as the song ends and I pull away from him. I grab my jacket and slip it back on before gathering my belongings.

I hear him following me before I even feel his hand wrap around my wrist. "Where are you going?"

"Home, I should have never come here with you. I'm giving my own self whiplash." I yank my wrist from his grip and turn back around.

"First of all, you can't drive. Actually, neither of us can drive right now so we'll have to call an Uber or something. Second of all, I'm confused as hell right now," Rathe says.

Frustration builds within the confines of my body. I run my hands through my hair but really, I want to yank it out. I want to scream at the top of my lungs. I don't do well with frustration. "That makes two of us. One minute I can't stand you. You're an ass and hateful. Then there's this confusing line of the fact we are teammates but also rivals. I don't even know what to do with that. The next minute you're staring at me with those chocolate brown eyes and I'm melting inside like some love sick puppy. I'm attracted to you in a way I've never been attracted to anyone before and I don't know what the hell to do with it. It's ridiculous."

Silence falls between us. My breathing is labored and the world is a little spinny thanks to the alcohol and now embarrassment. I swear I just keep embarrassing myself in front of him. It's becoming a problem. I open my mouth to apologize but when I look up Rathe is right in front of me. His mouth crashes down on mine. There's a hint of mint and whiskey on his tongue and I swear I get drunk just off his kiss. I dig my nails into his sides as an anchor because I'm pretty sure I'm about to float away. There's a split second where I think about how bad this could turn out. I have no reason to be kissing him. It'll just complicate things but then Rathe groans and I feel it all the way to my toes and I know it doesn't matter. I don't give a damn about the complications because for the first time in my life I feel like I'm home.

Twenty-One

Rathe

I could blame it on the alcohol. I should blame it on the alcohol but it'd be a lie. If I truly want to be honest with myself I've wanted to kiss Sutton from the moment she climbed out of the car and pulled her helmet off. Seeing her under that helmet shifted my world but it wasn't until right now that I realized that maybe that shift wasn't so bad. She's gotten under my skin and left me feeling open and vulnerable at times. I've been an ass as a defensive mechanism with her. She scares me off and on the track. I run my hands up her back until they tangle in her hair. God, she smells like heaven. She shouldn't feel this good, this right. Sutton is so soft everywhere which I guess in some way I didn't expect because she can out race most of the guys on the track. She's going to be my undoing.

Her nails dig into my ribcage and I press her back against the wall of the building. Sutton's words come back to me as her mouth molds to mine, as if it was always meant to be there. As if she is where I belong. I had no idea she was just as confused as I was about her feelings for me. Actually, I had no idea she had feelings for me at all but I'm damn glad I'm not alone on that battlefield. I've fought against every last feeling, thought and dream I've had about Sutton...until now. I'm not fighting anymore, I'm embracing them.

I grip her hands in mine and pin them above her head as I move my mouth to her neck. Her pulse is erratic and only causes the blood in my veins to pump harder. She moans and my grip tightens on her hands. All I can see or feel or smell right now is Sutton. Headlights flash across us and we instantly jump apart. I release her hands, reluctantly but when I look up the flush on her cheeks is all I need to remember what just transpired between us. She pulls her bottom lip between her teeth and I'm so tempted to step back into her and kiss those lips until the sun comes up in the morning but I know we can't continue that here. "I should go pay the bill. Will you order us an Uber?" I ask her. My voice is thick with lust and I can tell she knows it.

She nods her head and quietly replies, "Yeah, I can do that."

I stalk away without looking back, not because I don't want to but because I'm worried if I do that, I won't make it back inside to pay for our meal. I'll be too tempted to turn back around and claim every damn part of Sutton Pierce...just like she did me. The worst part is she doesn't even know it yet.

Twenty-Two

Sutton

The car ride was quiet and full of tension. Maybe it was sexual tension but I can't be sure in my current state. I can still feel Rathe everywhere. The rough skin of his hands against mine as he pinned me against the wall. His unwavering lips as he claimed my mouth in a kiss that would rival all other kisses. I've never been kissed like that before and I have this yearning to kiss him again. As I climb the stairs of the porch, I run my fingers through my hair, the breeze comes through and pulls Rathe's scent from my clothes, it invades my senses all over again.

I open the door as quietly as possible. However, a blinding light comes on as soon as I step inside. "Where in the hell have you been? I've been worried sick!" Evanna is pacing from the sound of her footsteps against the hardwood floors.

My head pounds and I cover my eyes. "Do you have to yell?"

"I'm not even yelling," she replies.

"Oh for the love of God please turn off the damn light," I complain as I turn around only to tumble into the wall and slide down until my butt hits the floor.

Evanna squeals which is what she always does when someone might be hurt. The light goes out and I hear her rushing towards me. "Sutton, are you okay?"

"Yeah but my ass hurts now so thanks for that."

"I'm sorry. I've just been worried. It's not like you to not be home at your normal time. I was worried something had happened to you. Where have you been and why do you look like a hot mess that was making out with someone?" I can hear the humor in her voice. She has no idea how correct she is.

My head drops back onto the wall and I take a deep breath. "I was at Pat's with Rathe…"

"Wait, Rathe, as in Rathe McCall? Your rival?" I can picture the shock on her face without even looking at her.

I nod my head yes. "The one and only."

"Okay, seriously, what the hell?"

The memories come flooding back and I can still feel the pressure of his lips on mine. I sigh. I'm not sure how to even explain this to Evanna. She's my best friend. She has literally been there through every single thing since my world was yanked away from me. Yet, I haven't told her about the attraction I've felt towards Rathe. I haven't told her about the dreams and thoughts that make my stomach flutter when I think about him. I've only told her how much I despise him and complained to her about how he's my rival and annoying. I don't know how to tell her about what happened tonight between us. I roll my head to the side and peek my eyes open. "We may have kissed…"

The light comes back on, temporarily blinding me. However, once I can see again, I'm very certain that if Evanna's eyes get any larger they will literally pop out of her head and roll across the floor of our house. The idea of her eyes rolling across our floor cracks me up and I start to laugh hysterically. Evanna is looking at me like I'm crazy now but then she begins to laugh along with me. After a few minutes she wipes the tears away from her eyes and takes a deep breath. "Oh, I get it. You were making a joke."

I could let her assume that and maybe I should but she is my best friend. Hell, she's like my sister and let's face it I need some kind of girl advice. "Actually, I wasn't. We totally kissed."

"What the…" Evanna doesn't finish her sentence as she slumps back against the wall, looking completely dumbfounded. "I didn't see that coming."

"You would have if I had told you what I've been thinking about," I admit quietly.

Her head whips back around in my direction. "Okay, you need to spill it now!"

"I've been attracted to Rathe from the beginning. I just didn't say anything. I felt like he was out of my league but then things changed today on the track. I helped him get over his fear a little I think. Hopefully, it'll stick and when we were leaving he asked me to go have dinner with him. I agreed and got a little drunk, danced, got caught up in the moment then tried to storm off only to have Rathe chase me down and kiss the hell out of me before he pinned me against the wall of the bar, my hands pinned above my head and made out with me like I was the air he breathed. It was hot and I don't know what the hell any of it means...if it means anything at all," I tell her, tossing my hands up in the air. I'm not completely sure she was able to follow any of that because I'm pretty sure I said it all in one breath and ran it together but she smiles at me like the Cheshire cat from *Alice in Wonderland*.

"I knew you two had something. I could tell the day he showed up to help us move our stuff."

"You could?" I ask. Evanna nods her head. "Well, you think next time you could fill me in, please?"

Evanna wraps an arm around my shoulder. "I could but where's the fun in that? Besides, you are both stubborn as hell so I knew the two of you would have to figure it out on your own. I'm glad to see it finally happened. So, tell me, is he a good kisser?"

She wags her eyebrows up and down as she waits for me to answer. I giggle in response. "He's so good, it should be illegal."

"Hmmm..."

I wait for Evanna to say more but she just gives me that grin that drives me crazy because it's like she knows something I don't. "What the hell does hmmm mean?"

"It means that the two of you clearly have more than a little rivalry going on. The two of you have some intense chemistry even if you both fight it and are trying to deny it. It's still there and we can all see it. Ryann and I talked about it for about two hours the other day," Evanna says casually.

"What?" I screech. "You and Ryann were talking about Rathe and I?"

Evanna rolls her eyes like I'm overreacting and I probably am. I mean I totally just had my tongue jammed down his throat so it's not like they're wrong but I've always just been a pretty private person by nature. It seems odd to have them talking about my non-relationship behind my back. "It wasn't anything bad. Ryann just asked me if I thought you might be into Rathe because she knew he was into you but he was fighting it."

"Did she really say she thought he was into me?" I ask like some silly school girl who just heard through the grapevine that her crush likes her back.

Evanna nods. "Of course, but that's not shocking, I mean what's not to like. Sutton, you're a catch. Anyways, I'm curious what's going to happen while the two of you are on the press tour together."

Now, it's my turn for my eyes to nearly bug out of my head. "What? Do you think something will happen?"

She laughs. "Yeah, most definitely. It'll be just the two of you the majority of the time. You guys will be in a different city, different hotel almost every night. Something will definitely happen. We should go shopping before you leave."

"Why? Revv-It will have an onsite stylist for every event that will dress me," I tell her as I attempt to stand up.

Evanna waves her hand in dismissal. "I'm not talking about regular clothes. I was referring to what you'll have on under the clothes."

"Aw hell," I mumble as Evanna helps me get to my room. She laughs. "I don't know if we'll even kiss again."

I fall back onto the bed and Evanna gets busy helping me strip my clothes off before slipping a t-shirt over my head. "I know you two will." Once I'm tucked in she heads out of my room, turning off the light as she goes.

"Evanna, I'm sorry for making you worry tonight," I call out to her.

She smiles back at me. "It's okay. It was worth the worry to see that smile on your face. Get some sleep because we are going shopping tomorrow!" She rushes out of my room as I groan and roll over to find a comfortable spot in my bed. As I drift off to sleep, I think about tonight and Rathe. I kind of hope Evanna is right and we do kiss again because I could live off Rathe McCall's kisses alone.

Twenty-Three

Rathe

It's been two days since I've seen Sutton and I can't even lie, it's driving me crazy. She's been on my mind every minute since that kiss outside of Pat's. She's consumed me. I'll see her today...finally. We'll be leaving for Detroit to kick off our press tour for Revv-It Racing in a couple of hours. I'm packing, last minute of course. The doorbell rings three times and I hear the echo as the door swings open and Maxton calls out, "Honey, I'm home."

I shake my head. "Upstairs dumbass."

About a minute later Maxton enters my bedroom with a shit eating grin on his face and two large cups from the local drink stop. "You wound me with your words when I come bearing gifts for you."

Rolling my eyes I reach out and take one of the cups from his hand. The fizzy soda loaded with vanilla and lime hits my tongue and soothes my growing nerves. I'm not even sure why I'm nervous. It's ridiculous because I've been around Sutton a lot these past few weeks but things are different since we kissed. "You're so dramatic. You might as well be a girl. No wonder you and Ryann get along so well."

A look flashes through Maxton's eyes but it's gone as quickly as it appeared so I let it slide. "Are you ready for the press tour?"

I shrug. "As ready as I ever am for these types of things."

"I can't even imagine. Listen, Ryann is worried about Sutton and this tour. Apparently, Evanna told her that Sutton is really nervous about all of it so can you, I don't know, be nice to her for a change." Maxton gives me the look that reminds me of a father.

He has no idea how nice I was to her a couple of nights ago. I start to feel defensive even though I shouldn't. I mean Maxton wouldn't be lecturing me if he knew I'd had Sutton pinned to the side of the building, exploring her mouth like some unknown land. "I've been nice lately."

Maxton rolls his eyes at my response. "Yes, for the most part. Could you be extra nice to her then?" I don't even reply as I turn around and head back into my closet to gather the last few things I'll need over the next couple of weeks. "What aren't you telling me?"

I take my time gathering the things I think I might need and even some I'm pretty sure I won't but it gives me more time to school my features. "What are you talking about?" I ask him as I come back out into my room.

"Don't play around with me dude. Something is going on so you might as well tell me now or I'll just find out later," Maxton says with that cocky grin on his face. I mean technically he's right but I don't want to tell him that. "So, what's her name?"

"Why do you think it has to do with a girl?" I ask. Defenses back up.

Maxton laughs. "Because you're Rathe McCall, of course, it has to do with a girl."

"You're wrong," I tell him.

He rolls his eyes at me. "If that's your story." Maxton's phone goes off and he fishes it out of his pocket. The grin that crosses his face catches me off guard. Maxton stands up abruptly. "I've got to get going but just remember to be nice to Sutton and keep your clothes on and your tongue to yourself while you're around her."

"What the hell is that supposed to mean?" I ask. My tone is harsh but I don't really care.

Maxton holds up his hands in surrender. "Just that I know you and I've seen how you look at Sutton but she's off limits, man."

"First of all, no one is off limits to me unless she says so. You don't get to dictate that. Second of all, I don't need your input."

I'm stalking away from him, towards my ensuite bathroom when I hear him clear his throat. "First of all, back the hell off man. I wasn't trying to give you my damn input. Also, Revv-It Racing can dictate what happens between the two of you."

"What?" I ask as I turn back around to face him.

Maxton shakes his head as if I'm missing the big picture here. "Did you even read your contract before you signed on the dotted line?"

My eyes narrow into a glare. Maxton might be my best friend but I'm not above beating his damn ass if he doesn't quit talking in damn circles. "Are you always this annoying?"

"Your contract says you can't have any kind of outside relationship with any member of the Revv-It Racing Team. If they are employed by the team they are off limits. Sutton is off limits. If you break the rule and they find out you could both be without a job." Maxton steps around me. Clearly, he's annoyed but I swear it's like he just punched me in the gut without even knowing. "Before you start the press tour where you're supposed to be a likable guy you might want to remove that stick up your ass."

I stand there long after he leaves. I hear the door slam shut behind him. When I can move again, I check the time and see I only have a few minutes before the car will be here to pick me up to head to the airport. I quickly zip up my suitcase and rush downstairs to my office. I rummage through my drawer of files until I find my Revv-It Racing contract. As I skim through it I'm praying Maxton is wrong. I mean I don't know what will happen between Sutton and I. There's a possibility it's nothing but if it's in our contract that we don't even get the opportunity to see, well it's going to suck. Finally, I find the portion of the contract that Maxton must have been talking about. Sure enough, it's there, in black and white. No two Revv-It employees can share a romantic relationship. Things must be kept completely professional. Both guilty parties will be released for breach of contract immediately.

"Shit!" I throw the contract across the room and watch as the pages scatter in the air and slowly fall to the floor. I signed this years ago without fully digesting what anything meant. I just saw the amount of the money I'd be making and signed my life away. Even if I had really paid attention to this portion of the contract I wouldn't have cared. There was no Sutton then. I would have never guessed she'd show up and turn my life upside down while fixing it all at the same time. A car horn from outside notifies me that it's time to leave. I gather my suitcase, my mind a jumbled mess and head out of my house, making sure to lock it up tight. As I slide into the backseat of the car all I can think is what in the hell am I going to do now? I've had a taste of Sutton Pierce and I don't think it'll ever be enough.

Twenty-Four

Sutton

I'm exhausted as I pull myself from my bed. I knew I would be, it was all part of Evanna's plan. She decided we should stay up as late as possible last night so I'd be tired enough to sleep on the plane today because I'm kind of freaking out over flying. Okay, not kind of, but totally freaking out. I've never been in a plane before and it's scaring the hell out of me.

It doesn't really help that I'm going to be seeing Rathe for the first time since we kissed. I'm not sure what to expect from him or our situation. It's dumb. I've never been a girl to worry about where I stood with a guy but it's different with Rathe.

Yesterday, I spent hours with Evanna shopping. We went to just about every store in the mall. I have an entire new wardrobe although I still say it's unnecessary. I mean I've also never been a girl to dress up or be concerned about lacy bras and underwear but apparently Evanna is. It took me a good two hours to get everything hung up and situated in my room and then another two to pack thanks to Evanna's help of unpacking basically everything I tried to sneak into my suitcase. She seems convinced that this press tour is going to be an excuse for things between Rathe and I to escalate. I completely disagree but I guess we'll see.

"You better have your ass out of bed," Evanna says as she barrels into my room. I sit up and give her a look that causes her to laugh. "Oh good, you're up!"

"Yeah, imagine that. Although, I will admit I feel like I got ran over by a semi at some point."

She hands me a can of cold soda and I take a huge chug. Is it ladylike? Definitely not. Do I care? Not in the least. "That's just how it feels after shopping for hours. You get used to it after a while."

I shake my head. "Nope, not me. I have enough clothes to last me ten years so I won't be shopping any time soon."

"You're such a strange girl sometimes," Evanna says as she plops down on the bed next to me. We sit in the quiet for a moment, listening to the clock on my nightstand tick away. "So, are you ready to go today?"

"I mean I'm packed but mentally I'm not anywhere near ready. I don't know what I'm more nervous about, the plane or having to see Rathe again."

Evanna rolls her eyes. "First of all, you'll probably sleep most of the plane ride so no need to worry there. As far as Rathe goes just act as if everything is normal unless he acts differently."

"Do you think he'll act differently?" I ask.

Evanna shrugs. "I don't know. He's hard to read. I do know that he's into you and I have a feeling he's going to want more than just one kiss."

"It wasn't just one kiss," I add.

She gives me a look. "You know what I mean. That being said I wouldn't be shocked if he reverted back to his ass hat ways. Guys like him have a hard time letting anyone in. They like to be in control and a girl like you throws them off their game. They fight against you and whatever they feel for you because they think it will be easier but in the long run they give in, hopefully before it's too late."

"A girl like me?"

Evanna nods her head. "Yep, a game changer. You are one of those girls who can change a guy's entire life if he lets you. They realize that pretty quickly but that also means they have to give up some control. They have to let you in and they get scared, whether they admit it or not. Eventually, they realize it's all a waste of time and they have to come back and ask for forgiveness."

Her thought process causes me to laugh. "That's a very detailed concept. I give you an A for effort but I'm not sure you're totally right. At least, not where Rathe is concerned."

"And why do you think that?"

I shrug. "I don't know. He doesn't seem like the type of guy to care about a game changer, as you called me."

"None of them give a damn about a game changer until they meet her. That's why it throws their world off for a while. They never see it coming until it's there," Evanna says it with a matter of fact attitude.

I nod my head. "If you say so."

"I don't have to say so. I know so. Anyways, things will work out however they are meant to with you and Rathe so for now don't worry about that. Just have fun and enjoy all these awesome opportunities. This is like a chance of a lifetime that you are being given so enjoy it." Evanna gives me the most encouraging smile.

I know she's right. I just always have this dumb little voice in the back of my head telling me I'm not good enough. I know it's technically wrong but it's still there and sometimes it wins. Sometimes, I really do feel like I'm not good enough. If I told Evanna she'd say it's a side effect of being in the system. Of ours parents neglect and abandonment that left us feeling like we don't belong or that we aren't good enough because they left us. Instead of telling her, I nod my head and agree. "You're right. I'll just try to enjoy it."

After our heart to heart Evanna and I get ready for the day. She's going to drive me to the airport and drop me off. I think she's worried if I drive myself or take an Uber that I'll end up not going. She could be right but I don't want to tell her that. I take my time getting ready. I slip on my favorite pair of medium wash skinny jeans, cheetah printed Converse and a red v-neck t-shirt. As I'm staring in the mirror, I decide to leave my hair down and let it do it's natural waves. Makeup has never been a big thing for me but I decide to swipe over a coat of mascara and some eyeliner before adding a pair of small diamond stud earrings. As I study myself in the mirror, I think I look like I have myself together even if I'm a mess on the inside. However, when they see me today, they will only see what I want them to see.

Evanna is in the kitchen making oatmeal when I finally leave my bedroom. The kitchen is large and a breath of fresh air compared to our old one. The new kitchen is white with pops of light gray and pale blue. We don't have a table for the dining room yet but we don't really need one because the island in the kitchen is massive, at least to us it is. All the appliances are new and stainless steel. Evanna slides me a bowl of oatmeal. "Eat up because we don't have a lot of time. By the way, you look great."

"Thanks," I tell her as I take a seat. We eat in record time. As we head through the living room and out the front door, we grab my luggage. I packed as light as possible since I'll have a stylist and what not for the events. Evanna and I pile into her new Ford Mustang and head for the airport. My nerves are at an all time high but I plaster the smile on my face to make her think everything is all good.

We pull into the parking lot and Evanna grabs the closest parking spot she can. She gets out of the car with me and helps unload my two bags. "I wish I could go in and wait with you but I know you'll be fine."

"Yeah, I'm fine. I got this."

Evanna smiles. "I know you do but it doesn't mean I'm not here to help."

I step forward and pull her into my arms. "Thank you Evanna. Thank you for being amazing. I wouldn't be doing any of this if it wasn't for you."

"Likewise. I love you Sutton. Be careful but have fun. Don't stress the small stuff," Evanna tells me.

I nod my head and give her a smile. "I will. You better be safe and if you need anything just call me."

She waves her hand dismissively. "I'm good. Now, go be a rockstar." I give her one last squeeze then turn around and head to the airport. I feel like I'm leaving every comfort I have in the world but I know it's got to be done. Maybe, this will turn out to be another great thing in my life.

Twenty-Five

Rathe

I'm staring at the windows, watching as the planes land or get prepared for take off. It's a beautiful day, sunny and clear, not a cloud in sight. However, the way I'm feeling on the inside is anything but sunny and clear. This morning I had been looking forward to spending time with Sutton over the next few weeks. Initially, I had thought we'd have time to get to know each other away from our normal surroundings without the pressure of friends or work schedule on the track but Maxton and that damn contract ruined that. Now, all I can think about is how she's off limits.

It's as if my body is somehow in tune with hers. I can feel her presence the moment she comes within a few feet of me. It's so strange because I seriously only thought that happened in those dumb romantic movies that Ryann used to make me suffer through. I never expected to actually experience it but here I am. I noticed it the first day on the track when every hair on my body stood at attention but I truly believed it was because she was my rival. I thought she was going to take my job and leave me in the dust. My assumptions were apparently wrong though.

I turn around and sure enough I see a stunningly beautiful Sutton standing there with a bag on one shoulder and another beside her looking nervous as hell. Maxton's words briefly play through my mind but my feet move on their own, towards her and by the time I realize it I'm standing in front of her. The tropical scent that seems to follow her is everywhere and those stormy blue gray eyes hold mine captive. How did I not see this coming the first day on the track? "Hi," I tell her. Mentally, I kick myself because it's been days since I last saw or spoke to her and the best line I could come up with was hi.

Sutton smiles even though it doesn't reach her eyes. "Hey, how have you been?"

I nod my head. "I've been good. How have you been?"

"I've been good." The air between us is thick with unease and tension. Neither of us knows what to say or how to act. I want to pull her into me and consume her, get lost in her kiss and forget about the outside world but I can't. It was done before it ever got started. I wonder if she realized the contract made us impossible too. "Actually, that's a lie. I've been a mess."

Her confession catches me off guard because Sutton doesn't strike me as the type to confess things easily. It's almost as if she's letting me inside the confines of her wall with one simple little truth. It's an olive branch of trust that I know not to take lightly. "What happened?"

Sutton takes a deep breath and looks past me out to the window where the planes are. "This happened. The press tour and airplanes. I never considered all this when I signed that contract. I just got excited that I could get Evanna and I in a better part of town and someone was going to pay me to race. It seemed like a dream come true but I never considered all of this."

Ironic, how the contract seems to have screwed us both over in different ways. "Look, I know the press tour seems intimidating right now but I promise after the first couple of stops, you'll get used to it. Plus, I'll be there, right by your side the whole time. I've done this a couple of times already so I got you. Also, they're going to love you."

"I don't know. I'm not the friendliest person. I'm not really a people person actually."

I shake my head. "I don't believe that. I think you have a guard up because of things you've gone through in your past but I think that people still love you Sutton. You draw people in without even realizing it. I mean Tucker saw it obviously. Maxton and Ryann too." I take a deep breath trying to decide if I want to add myself to the list. I want to, so damn bad but I also know that it doesn't matter what I want now. Why give us something else to hang onto when it can never be anyways.

"I hope you're right. That's not my biggest concern right now though." She pulls her bottom lip between her teeth. I've noticed her doing this before and I think it's just a nervous gesture but I've never wanted to kiss her before when she did it.

I clear my throat and try to shake the image from my head. "What's your concern?"

"Those damn planes."

Surely, I heard her wrong but then I remember Maxton mentioning her not being very happy over the planes earlier. I guess I forgot about that until now. After he told me about the clause in the contract, everything else kind of just flew out the window. "You've never been on a plane before."

Technically, I didn't ask her but she answers with, "No."

"It'll be okay. I promise. I know they seem intimidating too right now but I promise, you get used to them." I try to be comforting but it's never been my strong suit.

She gives me a smile. "Thanks Rathe."

Our pilot shows up and tells us we are ready to board our private plane. Sutton's eyes go large. I chuckle. "We get special treatment. It's the company's private jet. It's really nice and pretty damn comfortable too. Plus, there are things to entertain us. You won't even realize you're in a plane after a bit."

"I hope you're right." Jowanna, the media coordinator, appears in the area. She smiles and greets us both as she passes by. We follow her out to the jet and I take Sutton's luggage because it looks heavy and my mother would have the hide off my ass if I let her carry them. She tries to protest but I manage to wiggle them away from her. I feel the shock that comes off Sutton in waves as she steps into the jet. It's a bit extreme but it's awesome. All black leather seats, dark wood paneling, black and turquoise carpet with turquoise accents everywhere. It's truly a Revv-It Racing jet. There's a fully stocked bar, a large screen TV complete with a Blu-ray player and a private bedroom in the very back. I also happen to know there is a stack of board games stashed in the little closet in that bedroom. Chris and I loved to play games while on flights to help pass the time.

"I told you it was nice."

Sutton nods her head. "You weren't kidding."

"Nope. Grab a seat and I'll grab us something to drink." I head to the bar but decide to grab a soda or water from the mini fridge instead. Last time the two of us drank together we ended up making out with one another. Not that I'm complaining but that would definitely get both of us fired if we repeated in front of Jowanna. I can't take that chance and I doubt Sutton would either. Once I reach her seat, I hand her a bottle of water. "Do you like board games?"

Sutton gets a funny look on her face. I watch as she fidgets then looks away. "I never really played them but they seem fun."

"If you aren't into them, we can just watch a movie instead." I know board games are childish to a lot of adults. I find them fun and a good way to kill time but that doesn't mean she agrees.

"I really don't mind playing them. I just don't know a lot of them so you may have to explain the rules to me," she says.

I shrug. "I mean explaining the rules isn't a problem to me but you don't have to play just because I asked."

Sutton shakes her head. "That's not why I'm playing."

"Okay, I'll go grab some," I tell her as I stand up and head back to the closet. I grab Sorry, Clue, Checkers, Guess Who and Battleship and head back to the front. "So, let's start with Sorry. It's always been one of my favorites and I think you'll like it. Jowanna you want to play?"

She looks over and smiles. "No, I'm good. I have some work today but I'll definitely play Clue with you guys."

I give her a thumbs up and then I start to set up the game and explain it to Sutton. The smile on her face is easy and carefree. She's clearly already forgotten about the fear of the plane. After a couple of games Sutton starts to get drowsy because she decided to take a motion sickness pill because of her fear of flying. So, I help her back to the bed and tuck her in so she can sleep until we hit Detroit. When I come back to the main part of the jet Jowanna just smiles at me. "What?"

"I was worried the two of you wouldn't get along. I mean the two of you had a rough start there. It's just nice to see how you've both come so far." I nod and start to pick up the games. If she only knew just how far I'd come she might not think it's so great.

Twenty-Six

Sutton

I wake up with a jolt. I'm disoriented at first but things quickly come back. I'm on the Revv-It Racing private jet and I was getting sleepy so Rathe made sure I made it back here to the bed. I don't know how long I've been asleep but surely not too long. I stand up and stretch. There's a knock on the door that startles me but it's cracked open before I can cross the room and open it myself. Rathe's dark brown eyes find mine. "Oh good, you're awake. I was just coming to let you know that we're going to be landing soon so you need to come and buckle up."

"Oh good. I'm ready to be back on land." I run a hand through my hair hoping it doesn't look too crazy.

Rathe opens the door for me. "How'd you sleep?"

I shrug as I pass by him. "Pretty well, I think. That motion sickness pill that Evanna shoved at me seemed to really knock me out which is both a good and bad thing."

"Well, at least you didn't freak out on the flight. You looked so nervous before that I was a little worried." I can see the concern in Rathe's eyes when I look at him. It's not a look I've gotten often in my life so it makes me feel a little left of center.

I nod my head. "I was more than a little freaked out before but you helped distract me with the board games so thank you."

"I'm all about the service baby." He winks and my head falls back in laughter. At the mention of the board games I make a mental note to look up the rules for the ones he pulled out today. He seems to really enjoy them and I don't want him having to stop every time and explain how to play a new game. Besides, board games are usually a huge part of a childhood, if you get to

129

have a normal childhood. I never had a board game growing up. Evanna received Operation for Christmas one year. A local charity did an elf tree so people would pick an elf off the tree and buy a gift for the child. The elf would have the child's sex, age and things they enjoyed printed onto them. I don't know how but Evanna and her siblings got placed on to the tree one year. It was pretty much the only year that they really had a Christmas. I remember Evanna giving me one of her gifts to make me feel included. A few days after Christmas we were all playing Operation. Evanna's mom came barreling into the house and we all ran. We could tell by the wild look in her eyes that something was about to go down. We hid out in the living room closet and watched as one of her pimps came running in behind. He tripped over the game we had left behind on the floor. It quickly became the thing he used to beat Evanna's mom with. By the time everything was said and done and the pimp had disappeared the game was nothing but pieces. That was the last time I remember playing a board game. "Hey, are you okay?"

I shake my head trying to remove myself from the past. "Yeah, sorry I guess I spaced out a little. It must be a side effect of the pill."

Rathe accepts my excuse without further questions and I'm thankful for that. "Yeah, it must be. We should sit down." I allow Rathe to guide me back to the seat and I buckle up just as the pilot comes over the speaker telling us to prepare for our landing. I feel the panic start to rise in my gut and make its way through my body. I wonder for a split second if this is what Rathe was feeling on the track when he would suddenly slow down on the curve. I look over at him, studying his profile which is really too handsome for words. As if he can feel my eyes on him, he looks up. Our eyes hold onto one another and then I feel the warmth of his skin against mine as his fingers wrap around my hand, giving it a little squeeze of encouragement. "Just breathe," he says to me as I feel the shift in the atmosphere. My eyes stay locked on his and his thumb rubs back and forth over the back of my hand. It's soothing and calms the panic within me. Before I can even realize it we have officially landed. I let out a deep sigh of relief which causes Rathe to chuckle. "You did great Sutton."

"Thanks but I'm pretty sure you had a lot to do with that."

Rathe shakes his head. "No, that was all you." I stand up and go to grab my leather jacket I had left in my seat but it's gone. When I turn around, I see Rathe holding it open for me, waiting for me to slide my arms into it. I seriously only thought guys did this type of thing in movies but here Rathe is proving me wrong so I turn around and slide my arms into my jacket. Rathe's hands rest on my shoulder's for a few moments, I'm not sure why but it feels like something more. Maybe, the kiss is clouding my judgement. I've tried hard to keep my mind away from the kiss we shared a few nights ago. It hasn't been the easiest task but I've managed.

Jowanna turns around and Rathe's hands move away so quickly you would think that I tried to bite him or something. It's confusing. My feelings are a little insulted. I straighten my back and remind myself to act like nothing happened. If he's going to pretend, we didn't kiss then so will I. "Are you two ready to go?"

I nod my head and plaster on the brightest smile I can. "Yes, I can't wait."

I follow Jowanna off the plane with Rathe on my heels. I can feel his presence which is overwhelming and distracting but that voice inside my head keeps reminding me that it doesn't matter, that he doesn't matter. A large black SUV with black tinted windows is waiting for us outside of the plane and Jowanna quickly ushers us inside. Once we're on the road Jowanna starts to give us the schedule for the next couple of days. "So, tonight you will have the party for the launch tomorrow. It's at Club Dread. In your rooms you will find a few options for clothing. Hair and makeup artists will arrive at six sharp along with room service for eating. The limo will be outside and ready to go which also means you will be ready to go by eight sharp. You will play nice and meet a list of important people, take photos and be done by midnight. The limo will return you to the hotel then. Here is the schedule for tomorrow. I'm sure you can read and set your alarms accordingly."

I look at the schedule and once more the anxiety and panic start to build. "Will you be at the club tonight?"

"Yes, unfortunately I have to be present in case the two of you run into any issues that could cause us bad press." Jowanna gets sidetracked with her phone after that.

I look out the window to take in the city but I don't really notice much. My mind is reeling from all the information I was just handed. I'm trying to just breathe when I feel his eyes on me again. "You've got this. They're going to love you."

I scoff. "I'm not so sure about that but at least Jowanna is great at her job so if I mess everything up too bad, she'll be able to fix it and I'll be sent home."

"I won't let that happen. You'll do great. If we stumble into some odd territory just let me handle it. I've been in this situation before," Rathe offers.

"I don't need a babysitter." My tone is much harsher than I anticipated.

When I look over at Rathe, I can see he's caught off guard. He raises his hands in surrender. "I wasn't trying to imply that you did. I just remember how nervous I was on my first press tour and I was just trying to help."

I rub my temples as I feel the dull throb of a headache start to set it. "I'm sorry that was rude and I wasn't trying to be. I'm just stressed in general."

"No worries, I understand. If you decide at any time tonight you need my help or whatever, just let me know." Rathe turns to look back out the window. I feel like an ass but what's done is done. My bruised ego is making this harder than it has to be. Kissing Rathe McCall was a bad idea. Now, I need to learn how to separate everything and keep it strictly business.

Once we arrive at the multi-story hotel a bellhop appears and collects our luggage. Rathe and I follow Jowanna into the grand hotel. The lobby alone causes me to lose my breath. It's large and exquisite. High vaulted ceilings with a large silver chandelier hanging directly in the middle above a large, solid glass table with a bouquet of black and white flowers in the middle. The black tiled floor is so shiny you can see your own reflection. I'm so mesmerized by the beauty of the hotel that I don't even realize that Jowanna has already checked us in until a key is shoved into my hand and I'm told to follow her. We ride up the elevator to the sixteenth floor. Jowanna is a handful of rooms down from Rathe and I, who are next door neighbors. I swear I've pissed karma off at some point. That's the only explanation for this arrangement. I let myself into the room and the bellhop follows behind me to drop off my luggage.

I step into the room and it's just as amazing as the lobby. It's large and spacious, decorated in black, white and gray. The king size bed sits in the middle of the room beckoning me to just fall into it but I know if I lay down now, I'll never get up again. The large flat screen television is directly across from the bed. All the furniture is black and the gray carpet in the bedroom area is plush and thick. I take my shoes off and step onto it. Instantly, I sink into it, it feels just how I would imagine a cloud would feel. The far wall has white French doors that lead out to a small balcony. I can see the city beyond, it's mesmerizing. I never thought I'd see anything like this in my life. I turn on the TV and find something to give the room some noise while I unpack.

After unpacking I quickly climb in the shower before going to the corner of the room where dresses are hung on a bar and boxes of shoes, clutches and jewelry are scattered around the floor and desk. The bathroom is just as nice as the room itself. A large walk in, glass shower sits in the corner with a waterfall showerhead. The other corner has a white clawfoot soaking tub. Both call my name but I know to truly enjoy the tub I need more time so I decide to go into the shower. Once my skin starts looking like a prune I climb out of the shower and wrap myself up in the plush robe hanging on the back of the bathroom door before heading over to the clothes.

There are so many options and I already know I'll never be able to make a decision so I fish my phone out of my bag and Face Time Evanna. "Well it's about damn time I was starting to get worried about you."

Crap, I was supposed to let her know once we landed but I literally forgot. "I'm so sorry. I just got caught up and overwhelmed by everything around me."

"From what I can see of your room I'd say that's totally believable. So, how was the flight?" Evanna asks.

I shrug. "Better than I expected but still not my favorite thing in the world. So, I have to pick an outfit for tonight's launch party. It's a night club and I have a handful of dresses and accessories to pick from but I need help."

Evanna laughs. "Then you called the right girl. Show me what you got!"

Fifteen minutes later Evanna has my entire outfit planned for me. Each piece lying on the bed. "You're the best."

"I know it! Now, make sure you take a picture and send it to me once you're ready. I need to see my mad skills put to the test."

I shake my head and roll my eyes. "You're impossible but I love you anyways. Thank you for the help."

She waves her hand in dismissal. "You know I got your back. Go get ready. Don't forget my picture."

"Okay, okay, I will get you a damn picture."

Evanna blows me a kiss. "Love you boo!"

"Love you too." I end the call and turn to look at the outfit. It's not at all like anything I'd pick out for myself but I guess that's the point. This entire tour is me stepping out of my comfortable shell and moving into the new phase of my life. This is my life now. I take a deep breath just as I hear a knock on the door. I check the time and realize it's time to get this show on the road.

Twenty-Seven

Rathe

I'm more of a t-shirt and jean type of guy so having to get dressed up and let someone fuss over my hair isn't really my thing but I sit in the chair and play along like a good little boy. It's annoying as hell but I learned pretty quickly it comes with the territory. Once the girl whose name I've already forgotten, because Sutton is the only female on my brain lately, I stand up and study my reflection in the full body mirror. My hair is perfected into the messy style that is so popular right now, my beard trimmed close to my face and the black dress slacks with the midnight blue button up shirt completes the look along with my shiny black dress shoes. I suppose I look nice but I'd much rather be in my clothes.

I check the time and realize it's close enough to time that I can go ahead and make my way down to the lobby. As I'm making my way towards the door I decide to stop and spray just a little cologne. It won't make a lot of difference once I'm in the club but Sutton will definitely smell it on the ride over. There I go again acting like there's a chance for Sutton and I. The damn contract is haunting me now. Shaking my head I step out of my room and turn around to make sure my door is fully closed when I hear the door over from mine open. My eyes start at the feet where silver, sparkle heels are, traveling up toned legs until I reach the hem of a short, tight black mini dress. It has long sleeves and there is silver sparkle design throughout the dress. My mind is running a thousand miles a minute as it drinks in Sutton. She turns and I swear the world falls away. The dress may have long sleeves but the neckline is cut to mid-stomach. Large silver earrings and a silver choker complete her outfit. The silver makes her stormy blue gray eyes stand out even more. They hold me captive, hooded with dark eye makeup and shiny lips. She looks like perfection. You would never guess she was an Indy race car driver. She gives me a small smile. "You look nice." I know I need to say something but my mouth doesn't seem to know how to work. Her long dark hair is down and styled with simple, long curls. It's almost as if she's a different girl. Sutton cocks her head to the side. "Cat got your tongue?"

"You've got my tongue," I fire back without a second thought to the fire I'm playing with.

Her eyes widen just a centimeter but it's enough to let me know I still have an effect on her. "Yeah, sure I do."

Sutton turns to walk away but I reach out and grab her wrist, spinning her around to face me before pinning her back against the door. I feel the pounding of her pulse and how it spikes the moment our skin connects. I feel it strong, steady and beating frantically still as I move in closer to her. "You're always pushing me, testing me. It drives me crazy Sutton."

"And you're always playing this game of cat and mouse. One minute you're running away from me like I have the plague and the next you're jamming your tongue down my throat only to act as if it never happened the next time, I see you."

Our noses are almost touching. I can smell the scent of her shampoo, perfume and everything else that is Sutton. I don't need alcohol to get drunk. I can do that right here, pressed against Sutton Pierce, consuming her every breath the way she has somehow started to consume me. "I'm not playing a game."

I see the fire light in her eyes and she yanks her hands away from my grip and attempts to push me away but I don't budge. "You sure as hell could have fooled me."

"You just don't understand how dangerous this is for us. This is a literally a ticking time bomb that we're playing with," I tell her.

Sutton rolls her eyes. "You're so damn cryptic. It's ridiculous."

"This isn't me being cryptic or dramatic. It's the damn truth. That kiss did something to me but I can't allow it to go further than that and neither can you, trust me." I try to force her to see how badly it's killing me to say this. It's the last thing I ever want to say.

She shakes her head. "I don't trust people that I don't know and I certainly don't trust people who play games and talk in circles so no I won't trust you Rathe."

Her cheeks are flushed and I'm fighting the urge to reach down and stroke that silky skin. It's what I want to do so damn badly but I know I can't. Mentally, I'm killing myself because I took a bite of the temptation and now, I'm failing to resist. I should have never let Sutton close. I should have never let her help me on the track and I really shouldn't have kissed her because now it's all I want to do again. Screw my career, screw the contract, screw the world...which is all ridiculous because my career is all I have, all I ever wanted until my lips met hers. Without another moment of hesitation I claim her mouth in an aggressive kiss. Our lips mold together and I can feel her shock in her rigid muscles but slowly they release, her mouth opens ever so slightly, the invite I was looking for. I swoop in like a dehydrated man looking for water during a drought in Death Valley. My hands move to her hips, my fingers digging into her flesh. Sutton whimpers and I feel the last bit of self control I have break.

I'm reaching for my key when I hear another door open, down the hall. I jump away from Sutton as if a bucket of ice cold water was just dropped on me. We look like two hot messes, flushed, breathing heavily and guilty as hell. I smooth my shirt and wipe away the traces of Sutton that linger on my lips. Jowanna steps into the hallway in a leopard dress. She looks our way and smiles. "You both look great. Your outfits actually complement each other. I'm impressed." Neither of us say anything but we both nod in acknowledgement. Jowanna looks between us before nodding her head. "Are you two okay?"

I nod my head. "Yeah, we're great." I make a scene of checking my watch. "Shouldn't we get going?"

"Yes, of course," Jowanna tells us. I motion for Sutton to go ahead of me. She glares at me before stepping away from the door, taking the spot next to Jowanna. "I love your earrings."

Sutton smiles at her and it's one of those smiles that lights up the whole damn hallway. "Thank you. I love yours."

Jowanna raises her hand to feel her earrings. "Oh, thanks. I actually made these."

"Really?" Sutton asks, shock registered in her voice.

Jowanna shrugs. "Yeah, call it my side hustle."

"Do you sell them?" Sutton asks.

"Sure do," Jowanna replies and after that the entire ride down the elevator and in the limo to the club is these two talking about earrings. Normally, I'd want to jump out of the moving car and take my chances but I'm compelled to listen to Sutton, her questions and genuine interest. She's truly one of a kind and I'm in so much trouble and not just because of the contract. I don't worry about anyone but me and my family. Women are the last thing on my list of priorities but Sutton is quickly changing that and it's scaring the hell out of me.

Twenty-Eight

Sutton

My body is wired so tight right now that I'm afraid that if I look at Rathe, I might explode. He is so damn confusing. I thought I was the one being wishy washy but I think maybe it's him. Hell, who am I kidding? It's probably both of us. I'm just so frustrated. He watches me as if I'm some sort of magnet and he can't look away. He'll kiss me as if I'm the only oxygen around but then he acts as if he's embarrassed by me. I've been that girl enough in my life and I refuse to play that role for Rathe McCall. I've got to keep my defenses up with him because clearly, he and I can't be trusted together.

I listen to Jowanna talk about her earring business which is actually really interesting. She clearly enjoys it. I even pick out a few pairs for Evanna from the pictures on Jowanna's phone. I know she'll love them. When we arrive at the entrance of the club there are cameras everywhere and I feel my body grow even more nervous. "Okay you two, it's showtime. Now remember to smile and answer the questions. Pose for about four pictures then head inside. If they ask a question that you aren't sure about it, just give a vague, non-committed answer. It's the safest bet."

The back door of the limo opens and the crowd instantly turns in our direction. The flashes are blinding as the cameras begin to go off at lightning speed. Everyone is dying to get a picture of *the* Rathe McCall. He climbs out first and even though I can't see his face I can tell he's a natural. His muscles seem relaxed and he even gives the camera a little wave. As much as I hate to admit it I'm a little in awe of him right now. Rathe is waiting beside the door once I manage to climb out of the limo. He discreetly reminds me to smile which I do. The flashes from the camera are even worse outside of the car. All I can see are the nonexistent stars dancing in front of my eyes. Rathe's large, warm hand lands on the small of my back, guiding me to the entrance. When he stops to pose for a photo, I do the same. He stays beside me the whole time and even though I'm frustrated with him, at this moment I'm also completely thankful for him. I'm not sure I could have made it through this without his help, not that I'd tell him that.

Once we're inside the multi-story nightclub and Jowanna has joined us we are ushered to the VIP area where the Burnout Tire launch party is being held. Jowanna leads us as she follows the manager of the nightclub, going over the schedule and what not. Rathe stays close to me and I'm not sure if it's a good or bad thing now. I mean a part of me wants him close which is exactly why I should be running the opposite direction. Now that we're away from the flashing cameras and spotlight I feel more level headed. Inside the confines of the nightclub I can hold my own and stand on my own two feet without his help.

We head up a staircase until we reach a very private area. There is a bar along the far wall and a balcony to see the dancefloor below. The plush leather furniture looks more than comfortable. "There they are!" An older gentleman with a thick accent exclaims as we step into the area. His salt and pepper hair is slicked back but his almost black eyes zone in on me instantly. The creep factor instantly settles in the pit of my stomach and crawls up the spine of my back. Somehow Rathe must feel it too because I notice how quickly his spine straightens and as we move in closer, he purposefully places himself in front of me. The creepy guy, Raul, introduces us to the room of people. A lot of media and some of the Burnout Tire executives. I feel Rathe's hand on the small of my back again. I chance a look at him but all I can tell is that he is watching everyone around us. Oddly, enough I feel safe with Rathe.

As the night drags on, pictures are taken, drinks are ordered, bad jokes are told and things seem fine. Rathe hasn't left my side so I'm not surprised when he leans over and whispers into my ear. "I need to make a pit stop in the restroom. Will you be okay?"

I smile because it's sweet of him to ask even though he doesn't have to. "I'm good."

"I'll be back shortly." Rathe rises and I watch as he leaves.

I stand up, restless from sitting for so long and move to look over the balcony. One of the younger Burnout Tire executives, Trevor, comes over to join me. His smile is friendly and his blonde hair is cut so short to his head that he almost looks bald at times. "Finally, I get to talk to you."

I tilt my head out of habit. "What do you mean?"

"Rathe has been guarding you like you're his shiny new toy."

I shake my head and roll my eyes. "He has not."

Trevor scoffs. "He has and you know it. I can understand and respect it. This group of guys can be questionable at times especially when a beautiful woman is around. Plus, you're his teammate so of course he's going to look out for you. That's something I'm sure he learned from Chris."

"So, are you saying that you aren't like the rest of the guys in this room?" I question him.

"On many levels I am but not when it comes to women." Trevor and I talk for a good while, until my feet begin to ache from the heels I'm wearing. It's then that I realize Rathe has never returned and the worry starts to set in. I scan the club below, like I could possibly find him in the sea of bodies in the darkened room.

I abruptly cut Trevor off. "I'm sorry I need to go down to the ladies' room."

"No problem. Do you know where it is?" he asks.

I lie and say I do. Let's be honest Trevor is a nice guy but I don't trust him and I don't want him following me. Even if I really did need to use the restroom, I'm sure I could find it on my own. I turn on my heels and leave the VIP area. Once I reach the main floor I begin to search. At the end of the bar I catch a glimpse of a familiar shirt and I sigh in relief. However, my relief is short lived because as I get closer, I notice the girl sitting beside him with her hand resting on top of his. Some model type with a pixie haircut and a too lean body. Instantly, I feel embarrassed for being worried about him and coming to look for him. I knew better. I dig my phone from my clutch with the intention of calling Evanna but the time quickly stops me. There's a chance that she could be in bed, fast asleep, even though it's still early in California. Besides, she can't tell me something that I already know. I look back at Rathe and model girl one more time, burning and committing it to my memory before I turn around in search of the bathroom. It looks like I need some room to breathe after all.

Twenty-Nine

Rathe

I don't know what causes me to look up towards the balcony as I leave the restroom. Maybe, because my body seems to be so attuned with Sutton's. It's almost as if I'm subconsciously seeking her out at all times. It gets frustrating now that I realize what I'm doing. Before I kissed her I had no clue, it was easy to ignore the gnawing in the back of my brain telling me I was actually wanting her. After I kissed her there's a constant reminder that I can't shake. My mind stays wrapped up in her. It's distracting. So, when I looked up to the balcony and saw Sutton standing there with one of Burnout executive douche bags, that little green monster called jealousy reared its ugly head.

I spin around and stalk towards the bar. I need a damn drink and Revv-It doesn't like us to drink too much at events which I understand but these are unusual circumstances for me. The bartender quickly pours my double shot of whiskey which I down in two gulps. My intention is to return back to the VIP room but a woman who is nothing like Sutton comes up to me. By most standards she'd be pretty, maybe even gorgeous but right now to me, she's nothing. Nothing compares to the dark haired, blue gray eyed beauty currently standing upstairs flirting with some wannabe big shot.

The immature, prideful part of me wants to make her feel the jealousy I'm currently feeling in my veins. Sarah, the girl who came up to me, is a model and will do the job just fine. We quickly find a seat at the corner of the bar, tucked away from most wandering eyes. I keep an easy eye on Sutton from my seat on the stool. So, the moment she steps away from the balcony I expect to see her come downstairs. I've been gone long enough to make her wonder but there's a second there that I think she might not be coming down. Maybe, she isn't as concerned about me as I am with her. Maybe, it's completely one sided. Then I think back to the kiss we had just a few hours ago and I know better. I know it's not one sided, it's just not allowed.

Sutton is easy to spot, even in the darkened sea of people as she enters the main part of the nightclub. My eyes are instantly drawn to her but the moment she starts to scan the area I advert my eyes to Sarah. If she notices my quick change in demeanor she doesn't let on. If anything it encourages her. It never fails to shock me, even if it shouldn't, how quick the opposite sex will jump once they recognize you. This girl for instance is so desperate for my attention she's willing to settle for me when clearly my mind is somewhere else. It wouldn't take a detective to figure that out. All she would have to do is stop throwing herself at me and pay attention to what my actions are saying. She'd quickly follow my line of sight and see that I'm following Sutton's every move. However, Sarah doesn't care.

I can almost feel the shock that comes off Sutton when she discovers I'm sitting here with another woman. At first, I mentally pat myself on the back for accomplishing what I wanted. I wanted to catch her off guard but sadly I can't witness her reaction. I can't see if she's green with jealousy. However, when I look up and search out Sutton, I realize she's gone. My eyes continue to wander around the club in search of her until Sarah runs her fake fingernails up my arm. I pull away and turn back to look at her. "I should get going."

She gives me a coy smile and normally I would be overly excited about this but not tonight. "Where are you going? We're just getting started."

"Maybe you're just getting started but I'm leaving." I stand up and start to walk away when her hand wraps around the belt loop in the back of my pants, pulling me back towards her.

"Are you wanting to be chased? Is that the game you like?"

I shake her hand off and spin around to face her. She really thinks I'm trying to play with her right now. "I'm leaving. It's not a game. It's not a joke. It's not anything except that this isn't happening."

She pouts her lips which are probably just as fake as she is. "Baby…"

I hold my hand up to silence her. "No, move along." I stalk away from Sarah and head straight back to the VIP room. Jowanna is busy on her phone as always but it's Sutton that shocks me. She's in the middle of the executives. The young one that she had been talking with at the balcony is sitting beside her, too close if you ask me. His hand on her knee. Laughing and carrying on a conversation. She's clearly not nervous anymore. Jealousy surges through me once more.

As I look around it seems like maybe I made a fool out of myself by trying to protect her from the creepy man earlier. Maybe, I misread her reaction because she certainly seems comfortable now. I grab a beer and make my way over to them. I take a seat towards the outside of the group and Sutton smirks in my direction. Son of a bitch, I missed it all. She's been up here winning over the executives of a tire company. Securing her spot in the Indy racing industry. She's playing the role she gets paid for while I've been running around trying to make her jealous, losing my chance to get the executives on my side. I can daydream about Sutton all day long but at the end of it…she's my rival.

****

The limo ride back to the hotel was quiet. It felt tense to me but I doubt Jowanna noticed since she was busy on her phone the whole time. When we pull back up to the hotel Jowanna looks up. "You guys did great tonight. Don't forget to set your alarm for tomorrow and memorize your script before you get there."

Sutton and I both nod. Neither of us look at the other one. The three of us take an elevator up to our floor. Jowanna says good night as we pass by her and she ducks into her room. Sutton and I, alone in the hallway, however things are so different from where they were a few hours ago when I had her pressed against the door. My mouth molded to hers in a way that I've never experienced before. Now, there might as well be an entire ocean between us.

We reach Sutton's door and she slips her key in and waits for the light to flash. She looks over her shoulder. "Good night Rathe." She disappears inside and I'm left standing in the silent hallway, staring at the door that is currently keeping me from what I want. I pace the floor a few times before I cross the hallway and go into my own room. I need to get to my shit together and forget about these feelings I have developed towards Sutton. Standing under the scalding hot water of the shower I try to list the reasons why I need to forget about this attraction I have for Sutton. I stand there repeating the same few reasons over and over until the water runs cold. Finally, I step out and pull on a pair of clean gym shorts before heading to the king size bed.

As I pass the connecting door of our rooms I pause. If I could just explain to her why I've been so hot and cold maybe then she'd at least understand but would it really do any good? I run a hand through my damp hair. I swear I have never been this way over a girl before, not even when I was a teenager.

I'm standing there trying to decide what I should do when there's a light tap on the door. So light I wonder if I've imagined it. I move closer and wait to see if it happens again. A few seconds later another light tap. I unlock the door and open it.

Sutton stands there in a pair of tight red shorts, that cling to her body like a second skin and a black tank top. Her hair is still down but her makeup is gone. She looks even more beautiful than before if that's possible. Her nose is currently buried in a stack of papers so she hasn't even looked up yet. I'm allowed a few moments to just study her. "How am I supposed to know which part I'm supposed to say tomorrow?" She looks up, a perplexed look on her face. Her eyes widen as she takes in my appearance. "Oh goodness, were you sleeping? I didn't even think about that."

I shake my head. "I wasn't sleeping. I just got out of the shower. Is that tomorrow's script?" She nods her head yes, her eyes still wide. "Your part should be highlighted."

"There's nothing highlighted," she says as she hands me the papers.

Sure enough nothing is highlighted on her copy. "I haven't checked mine. Come on in," I tell her as I cross the room to the desk where the stack of papers are. I pull mine out and see my lines highlighted. "Let me call down to the front desk and see if we can borrow a highlighter so we can highlight your lines for you."

"You don't have to do that," she comments. She is barely standing inside my room, fidgeting with her hands.

"How else are you going to learn the lines darlin'? Also you can come inside the room I don't bite...too much." I give her a big smile and she shakes her head.

"I think it's safer for both of us if I stay over here."

I cross the room until I'm directly in front of her. Toe to toe and nearly chest to chest. "Why would you say that?"

Sutton looks away. "Because this game is getting old."

I reach out and lightly trace her jaw with the tip of my finger. "I told you earlier this isn't a game."

"Sure it isn't," she shoots back. "I'm not some star stuck girl you know?"

I chuckle. "Believe me, I know that darlin'."

Suddenly, a little frustrated growl escapes her. It's one of the cutest yet sexiest things I've ever heard. "Don't call me darlin'. I'm not some dumb bar bimbo you can toy with Rathe."

"Dumb bar bimbo? Do I detect some jealousy?" I tease her but inside I'm on cloud freaking nine. I wanted to make her jealous and it worked. She feels this too otherwise she wouldn't have gotten jealous. I take a step forward and she steps back only to hit the wall behind her. "I wanted you to get jealous. I wanted to see that little green monster in those stormy blue gray eyes."

"And you say this isn't a game." She scoffs and tries to push me away but I don't budge.

"It isn't a game. When I saw you on the balcony flirting with that executive douche bag, I got so jealous I wanted to rip his hands off his body so he couldn't touch you. I'm drawn to you even if it is against the rules. I need to know if you feel it too." Her eyes watch mine, never wavering and in a split second, rash decision her mouth is fused to mine. Our hands claw at one another and the world slips away. It's just her and I and how quickly we can become one.

Thirty

Sutton

I wake up to the sound of knocking on the door and a warmth beside me that I don't understand. Then I roll over and smack my face into the chest of Rathe and I everything floods back. I sit up taking the sheet with me while shaking Rathe. "We forgot to set the alarm and I think Jowanna is knocking on my door."

Rathe sits up quicker than I've seen anyone move before in my life. Don't forget I've seen Evanna going on Black Friday sales so to say Rathe is moving faster than her is really something. He's out of bed with his shorts on before I can even blink. "Stay here, let me handle this, please," he says as he runs into my room, closing the connecting door on his way. I barely catch a glimpse of the artwork that takes up his back before the door closes. The moment I saw the tattoo I was curious about it but I have yet to get a good look at it. I climb from his bed quietly and slip my clothes back on. As I'm getting dressed the door opens and Rathe reappears. "What was that all about?"

"Jowanna just reminding us that we need to be ready for hair and makeup in an hour and breakfast is being sent up." Rathe looks nervous. That little stress line between his eyebrows is clearly visible and the muscles of his body are obviously tense.

I continue to study him. "That's great but why shut the door between the rooms?"

Rathe scans the room as if he's looking for something but I know he isn't before shrugging. "Oh but if she asks, I switched rooms with you because the people next door were so loud and you were already nervous and couldn't sleep."

The fact that he's making up stories about why I was in his room makes me uncomfortable. Instantly, my defenses go up and I feel my attitude shift. "Why would I need to make up a story for why I was in your room?"

"Because that's what I told Jowanna," Rathe says as he busies himself by digging through his luggage.

"Stop avoiding me," I say harshly. Rathe looks up, shock registered on his face. Clearly, he didn't expect me to question him. "Why did you tell her a story?"

"It was necessary."

I scoff. "How was that necessary? I mean we were two consenting adults the last time I checked so why in the hell would you need some made up story?"

Rathe runs a hand through his hair and I remember the feel of it last night between my fingers. My body instantly reacts as the memories from last night come flooding back. He scrubs his hand over his face and dread settles in my gut. I'm clearly missing something here and I want to know what it is. "I didn't make up the story because I regretted it or didn't want her to know...it's because she can't know."

"What the hell is that supposed to mean?" A thought takes over my mind causing me to cringe. What if I'm the other girl? What if he has something going on with Jowanna? "Oh my god! Do you have something going on with Jowanna?"

Based on the look of utter disbelief on his face I'm going to say my assumption is wrong but I need to hear him say it. "No, Jowanna is a great person and beautiful but there's nothing going on between us."

"Then what is the problem?"

"Damn it, Sutton! It's in our damn contract! There's an entire clause stating that two Revv-It Racing employees can't have any non-professional relationship. Both will be automatically terminated if caught, no questions asked." Rathe paces the room back and forth like a caged animal.

"What?" I whisper as all the blood in my body goes rushing to my head. The sound of my pulse vibrating in my ears.

"I didn't know about it the night I kissed you. Maxton reminded me of it right before we left to come here yesterday. It's why I acted so differently. I never really read the damn contract. I was young and just saw the amount of money I'd be making and signed on the line. This wasn't planned." Rathe is standing in front of me now, reaching for my hands but I can't let him do that anymore.

I can't find comfort in him. I can't let him guide me through the tour because I'll only continue to fall for him. There's no way I can afford that. If I fall anymore there's no going back. I take a deep breath and swallow past the acid burning my throat because the next words I say are going to be so hard. "Last night was a one time thing. Call it a mistake. From here on out we will be nothing but professional. You take care of you and I'll take care of me."

"Sutton..." his voice is quiet and I can hear the silent plea in his tone. It pulls at my heart but I can't risk this career now.

I take a deep breath and cross the room to the door. "We go back to being rivals," I tell him before I step into my room and close the door.

Thirty-One

Sutton

This past week has been like living in hell! Trying to ignore Rathe, his presence and the way my body reacts to him is damn near impossible. It's been miserable. If it wasn't for Evanna keeping me sane via FaceTime I don't know how I would have gotten through it. I sigh and fall back on the bed. Tonight is our night off at least, the first one since we started this tour.

I stare at the sky blue ceiling of yet another hotel and remind myself I have one week down and one week left to go. Starting tomorrow I can really start a countdown until I'm back home. The only good thing I can say is that at least I have managed to learn how to handle the anxiety of flying.

Grabbing my phone I send a quick text to Evanna telling her to call me in about an hour. I unpack what I'll need for the night before I grab the menu from room service. I'm starving and everything sounds amazing. My stomach growls angrily at me just telling me to pick something. I end up ordering an entire pizza and soda. Once I double check to make sure everything that has to be taken care of is, I start the shower to let it get good warm before hopping in.

The warm water caresses my skin and instantly my mind goes right back to the memory of Rathe's hands on my skin. "Damn it!" This has been the biggest problem. I can't ignore him. I can't ignore that night and the damn memories. I can't ignore the way he makes me feel or the fact that I've been weighing the pros and cons of actually jeopardizing my contract. It's crazy and I know it but Rathe brought out something in me I didn't know existed.

The water starts to cool and I hop out of the shower and dress quickly in my shorts and tank top just as there is a knock on my door. Opening it up I see a hotel employee dressed in uniform with my soda and box of pizza. "Thank you so much," I tell him as I take the food from him. "Let me grab your tip." That was never something I thought about until the second hotel of our tour. The guy just kept standing there and for some reason the scene from Pretty Woman came to mind and it dawned on me that he was waiting for a tip. Now, I've tried to be more mindful of it.

"Here you go. You have a nice night." His smooth voice has my body instantly reacting. I spin around to see Rathe slipping money into the employees hand. His sweats hanging low on his hips and the muscle tank hugging every inch of his body. "A whole pizza? All to yourself?"

This is the first time since I left his room, declaring us rivals once more, that we've been truly alone. The first time that we've really spoken to one another. Well, I guess I haven't spoken but he did speak to me. "What are you doing here?"

He shrugs as he steps into the room, letting the door shut behind him. "To be honest I'm not really sure. I shouldn't be here, I know that. I guess between the two of us, you're the stronger one."

I shake my head. "That's not true."

Rathe cocks his head to the side and takes one hand and scratches at his beard. The sound fills the room. "Isn't it though?"

"Why would you think that?"

The low, throaty chuckle that comes from him sends shivers down my spine. "I thought that was obvious. I mean staying away from you these past few days has been a form of torture I didn't know existed. Watching you laugh, smile and talk to all these other guys, even if it's for the press drives me crazy with jealousy. Sitting on the jet, so close to you, yet so far away. It's like I'm close enough to reach out and touch you but I'm not allowed."

"Did you ever think maybe that's part of the problem?" Rathe's eyebrows pull together in confusion. "We're not allowed. Maybe, that's the big draw for you. Maybe, it's wanting what you can't have."

Rathe shakes his head. "I'm not that type of man Sutton. I don't give a damn about what I can't have. I just move on to what I can have. I don't like wasted time."

I sigh. "That's great but you shouldn't be in here."

"It doesn't bother you at all, does it?" he asks. His eyes are full of curiosity and another emotion that I can't pinpoint.

"What are you talking about Rathe?" I'm so lost. I feel like I'm not really an active member in the conversation right now with the way he's changing subjects.

Rathe moves in closer to me and I swear it's like the air automatically gets thicker and the room shrinks a couple of sizes. His presence is always so commanding. "It kills me to keep my hands off you, to stay away from you. The taste of your kiss haunts me but you're perfectly fine."

The laugh that bubbles out of me is anything but joyful, it's sarcastic as hell. "Fine? You think I'm fine?" Rathe shrugs. "You're an idiot! I'm anything but fine. Everything about you and that night haunts me. I can't be around you without feeling this flutter in my stomach which is annoying as hell and it makes it hard to eat which pisses me off because as soon as I'm away from you I'm starving. It's why I have to order a whole damn pizza for myself! I want to yank every bimbo's extensions from her damn head when I see you talking to them because I'm so jealous and I don't get jealous but I swear I'm the color of that witch from that movie with the ruby red slippers. I'm going crazy trying to ignore it all and smile through it and act like nothing's wrong! I'm so not fine Rathe!"

Rathe's hands wrap around my wrist and yank me into him. I tumble into his chest and his hands wrap around my waist holding me to him. His warmth invades me. His scent is everywhere and makes my head feel foggy. "It's about damn time woman." His mouth comes down on mine hard and fast. This kiss is anything but soft or tender. It's rough and bumpy but so necessary. All the frustration over our current situation is fought out in this kiss, in the way our teeth accidentally bump, our tongues dance and our lips mold. It's everything and not nearly enough all at once. This is everything we can't have but everything we need wrapped up in one messed up situation.

My pizza and soda are forgotten as I fall back onto the bed, pulling Rathe with me. Neither of us are willing to let this moment go. We refuse to break the kiss in fear that it will break this moment between us. If our lips stay sealed to one another then we can fight reality, keep it at bay. There's no contract or clause or career between us right now. It's just Rathe and I, skin to skin, breath to breath, heartbeat to heartbeat.

Thirty-Two

Rathe

I wake up to aches in my muscles that I haven't felt in a while. The warmth besides me startles me at first but then as I look over, I see Sutton. Watching her sleep is much more fascinating than it should be but I watch as her bare back rises and falls with her slow and even breathing. Her dark brown hair fanned over the stark white pillowcases. The little flutter of her eyelashes. My hands itch to touch her. None of this makes sense. I barely know her yet I crave her on such a different level from anything I've ever felt before. That yearning in the pit of my stomach and dead flat in the middle of my chest. I could have never predicted Sutton.

I move to my side and lightly trace my fingertips up and down her spine lazily. There's a scar over her right shoulder blade and I want to know the story behind it. I want to know it all. Frustration settles within my soul because I can't know it all. I shouldn't even be here right now. The contract that ultimately gave me my life is also quite possibly ruining it. To have Sutton right next to me but completely untouchable is my own personal hell that I could have never prepared for. I'm so close to saying screw the contract. I've made more than enough money to live comfortably for years, if not for the rest of my life. I could manage just fine but then I know I can't. I'd miss the thrill, speed and adrenaline. The three things that I just got back, thanks to Sutton. How do I walk away from the only thing I've ever known? Is it worth it? I'd be walking away for a woman who I don't even know. We have no history and no ties to one another aside from racing. There's no guarantee she'd stay or that she even feels the same way I do at the end of the day. Plus, it wouldn't just be my career I'd be ending....it'd be hers too.

I sigh and roll back to stare at the ceiling. Time passes but I don't seem to notice until I hear the growl coming from Sutton's stomach just before she stirs. My head rolls to the side as she opens her eyes. "Well hello beautiful."

The blush floods her cheeks and she closes her eyes. She really doesn't take compliments well. "Hi," she says quietly. Her stomach rumbles again and she groans as she buries her face into the pillow. I laugh because I can't stop it. "I'm so hungry."

"I caught that," I tease her. "It might be because you've barely eaten all week."

She brings her face back to look at me and runs a hand through her hair. "I've eaten just when I'm alone. When I'm around you it's too hard. Everything is just...more."

The honesty in her eyes shocks me. She truly means that. The selfish bastard I am eats up her words as if they will be my last. "Is that why you ordered a whole pizza?" She nods her head. I sit up and reach for the room's phone.

"What are you doing?" she asks. I feel the bed shifting beside me. She comes to stand in front of me a few seconds later, her discarded shorts and tank top back in place. She watches as I order two fresh sodas and side of ranch dressing. When I hang up the phone, she shakes her head. "I can't believe you are going to ruin the best food in the world with ranch dressing."

"Darlin' I'm not ruining anything. I'm enhancing it and I'm not sure you can classify pizza as the best food in the world."

"Oh, I can and I did and you are in fact ruining it. It should be criminal the way society slaps ranch dressing on every single thing nowadays," she says as she stalks across the room and turns the lamp light on.

I laugh as I pull my shorts on. "What is your issue with ranch? I mean seriously, what did it ever do to you?"

She shrugs. "I'm allergic to it."

I feel like my jaw is on the floor right now. That wasn't what I was expecting. "I didn't even know it was possible to be allergic to ranch."

Sutton rolls her eyes and grabs the pizza box and starts placing pieces on paper plates. "It's possible to be allergic to anything, I think anyways." A knock on the door causes her to jump and I chuckle. I go to answer it but she pushes me back behind the wall. The look on my face must show my shock. "You aren't supposed to be in here right?" I nod as the issue settles between us. She opens the door and collects the sodas and ranch. After the pizza is reheated and we are seated in bed watching Pretty Woman on the TV Sutton looks over at me. "Why didn't you tell me?"

"Tell you what?" I ask. I think I know what she's referring to but I should be sure before I answer.

She wipes her hand on a napkin. "About the contract."

I shrug. "I just figured either you knew and didn't care or you didn't know and it would be best if I was just an ass to you. I could make you hate me, make you forget me and then it wouldn't matter."

Sutton shakes her head. "Your logic is dumb. I could never forget you. I doubt I could hate you."

"So, why are we watching Pretty Woman?" I ask.

She smiles at me when she turns towards me. "Because it's one of my favorite movies but hardly anyone knows that so don't go advertising."

"Really?"

Sutton nods. "Yeah, I mean every girl dreams of her knight in shining armor coming to rescue her. Even the strongest, most independent woman in the world still wants someone to care about her. We all want to know that we matter to someone." I study her and there's a sag in her shoulders and sadness in her eyes right now. Something or someone has made her feel like she didn't matter and I hate that. I want to fix that. "What are we going to do Rathe?"

I don't have to ask what she means because I know. She wants to know what we are going to do about us. My hand reaches across the bed in search of hers. Her slender hand finds mine, halfway. "I don't know for sure. I know what I want but it doesn't agree to the terms we signed on for. We could always keep it a secret and see where it goes."

"And what? We act like rivals in front of everyone else?" she asks.

My thumb caresses the soft skin on the back of her hand. How do women's hands always feel so unbelievably soft? "Yeah, we could. I mean at least until we find out what we want from one another. I know we both want to race but I can also tell we both want this to a certain extent too."

Sutton takes a deep breath and releases it slowly. "You're not wrong. So we sneak around and keep this quiet but still act like we always have in front of everyone else."

"That's the best I can come up with. It's juvenile but it's all I've got." I give her an apologetic look.

I can see her brain processing it all so I collect our now empty plates in the trash and clean up any mess we made. I don't climb back into the bed, I just stand beside it and wait to see what she wants to do. "I don't have any other solution either so we'll just have to make sure we're careful."

"We'll be very, very careful."

Sutton gives me the smallest smile. "Well, can we set the alarm earlier so that way you can stay here until then?"

My chest warms with her request. "Anything you want darlin'." I climb back into the bed and Sutton lays beside me. She falls asleep long before I do. At some point she stirs and before I realize it her head is on my chest. I've never been one to cuddle. I'm not even sure I've held someone like this before but with Sutton, it just feels right.

Thirty-Three

Sutton

When I wake up Rathe is gone and the sun is coming through the windows. It's scary how my heart sinks a little at his absence. I mean in retrospect we don't even really know each other but there's something about him that makes me feel safe and that's not something I'm used to feeling. As I roll over, I check the time and see my original alarm will go off in about ten minutes so I decide to get a little head start. Today, Rathe and I, will be at a grand opening of a miniature Indy track for children. It's basically a go-kart track but it looks a lot fancier, at least in the photos that I've seen. Luckily, I won't have to be overly dressed up for this event and I look forward to hanging out with some of the kids.

Over the next two hours I'm fed, primped and dressed with just minutes to spare before I have to head down to catch the ride with Rathe and Jowanna. I take a minute to just breathe. My room has been a flurry of people and I'm going to enjoy the quiet for a moment. I look in the mirror and at least I can kind of recognize myself today. Black, distressed skinny jeans hug my legs with a grayish blue satin tank and black leather jacket. I tried to insist on wearing a pair of Converses but the dream team as they call themselves refused so I now have some black high heels on with the outfit. They pulled my hair up into a messy ponytail which I'm sure I'll be grateful for once I'm in the Florida heat. My makeup is on the light side too. My cell phone pings and I know it's time to go so I grab my clutch and head out into the hallway.

I'm pulling my door shut when I hear the low whistle come from behind me. When I spin around, I'm shocked to see Rathe, looking like sex on a stick, leaning against the wall. His dark eyes roam my body and instantly my skin prickles in anticipation. I'd give almost anything to cross this hallway and pull his mouth to mine, kissing the hell out of him. Sadly, that is not an option. He looks illegally good. His light wash denim jeans hang low on his hips with a simple black t-shirt hugs his biceps. The aviator shades that he seems to love so much are tucked into the collar of his shirt and I'm envious of his shoes. "Why do you get to wear normal shoes?"

Rathe chuckles. "Because there's no way in hell I could pull those off, let alone walk in them."

"Yeah, well I can't exactly walk in them either but they keep throwing them on me," I say as I roll my eyes.

Silence falls between us and when I look up the heat in Rathe's eyes is almost my undoing. His teeth have sunk into his plump bottom lip as he watches me. "I'm kind of glad they do. You make them look damn good. Although, you could probably make anything look good."

I scoff and roll my eyes. "Yeah, sure." The elevator dings in the quiet hallway and I move towards it. We're going to be late if we don't get going. I hear Rathe behind me but I know I have to act normal so I don't turn around to see where he's at. I don't really need to because my body seems to be hyper aware of his presence.

I move to one corner and Rathe moves to the other corner but I can feel his eyes on me. "You really don't see it do you?"

Are there cameras in these elevators? I want to look at him so badly but I know I shouldn't. "See what Rathe? You're talking in circles again," I tell him as I raise my head, giving him a look that I've often given him in the past.

"How damn gorgeous you are," he says. It's so quiet I'm not even sure I heard him right. I'm stunned into speechlessness and by the time I finally find my voice the elevator doors slide open and Jowanna is in front of us.

"It's about damn time. I was fixing to come back up there."

I shake off Rathe's comment. "Sorry, you know Rathe. He's always got to have that extra beauty time," I tell her with a roll of my eyes as I step out of the elevator.

Rathe chuckles and I can hear the extra sarcasm he's added for Jowanna's benefit. "Well, I'm so sorry I don't have a whole glam squad to make me presentable to the general public."

I make a point to bite back the smile threatening my face right now. "Ha-ha, you're so funny," I tell him.

"That's enough!" Jowanna swings around to stare us down. She's got that mom look about her right now and it's a little intimidating. "I know you two have this competitive type of relationship that is super annoying and unnecessary if you ask me but stick a cork in it. Today, I don't want to deal with it. Just go back to ignoring each other if you have to but can the two of you at least pretend to be nice to one another for today?"

Rathe and I exchange a glance but it's so much more. Who knew a brief glance could say so many things at one time? "We'll call a truce for today to make it easier on you," Rathe tells Jowanna in his silky smooth voice.

"Yeah, I know I'm sorry. We're not trying to make your job harder." There's a chance that Rathe and I are being a little over the top and I'm crossing my fingers that Jowanna doesn't catch on.

Jowanna eyes us carefully, trying to decide if she believes us or not. Finally, she nods her head, causing her dark bob haircut to bounce. "Alright, good. Then let's go do this thing."

The ride to the Go-Kart Indy track is a quiet one but I felt Rathe's eyes on me more than once. I didn't need to look his way to know I was right. The heat of his stare was all I could feel. Ignoring him was going to be nearly impossible. When we pull up to the track, I see a large crowd of people, many of them press. We all climb out of the car. Rathe and I are stopped for questions and pictures. We even sign a few things. I never thought I'd be asked for my autograph. It was certainly a surreal moment for me.

Once we make it past the fence and into the actual track area I see a line of kids, dressed like miniature Indy race car drivers, standing next to their cars. It's one of the cutest things I've ever seen and for some reason I grab my phone and snap a picture of it. We are introduced to the owners of the business before being ushered onto the stage where we give our speeches. My speech is short and sweet. I don't have a lot to say because as I was growing up my only goal was to survive. I didn't consider racing or anything else. It was just about making it out of the system, getting a job and trying to find my place in the world. Racing came into my life much later than most of the kids standing behind me. However, as Rathe takes the microphone I can tell by the look of passion in his eyes that his speech is going to be the crowd pleaser.

"Growing up cars were everything to me. My father worked forty plus hours to ensure that my mom, sister and I had everything we could ever need and most of what we wanted. He went to work early and came home late. A lot of the time I missed his presence at our dinner table or during a movie on our couch but he always made it a point to be home on the weekends. At first, I tried my hand at sports like so many young boys do. I wanted to impress my father and he never missed a game even though it was obvious that football, soccer and baseball were not my passion. Then one weekend I found my father in the garage of our home. There was this beat up, old car, basically a piece of junk sitting there and the look in my father's eyes shocked me. He looked so proud of this car. I remember asking him about it and he told me the story about his father and a car he had just like this one sitting in our garage. Something about the way he told the story made me want to be part of it. I asked my father if I could help him and of course he told me yes. Sports quickly became a thing of my past. Every weekend we'd spend hours in that garage, fixing that piece of junk up. Then one day I walked into the garage and realized it wasn't a piece of junk anymore but a work of art. We ended up having the car completed within a year. My father took the whole family out for milkshakes and we cruised around town. Two years later on my sixteenth birthday he slid the keys into my hands and told me it was mine now. It was the day that changed my life because before I slid behind the wheel of that car, I wanted to be a mechanic. However, the moment I pulled out of the driveway of my childhood home and pushed the gas pedal down, the wind hit my face and the feeling of freedom sat in my bones, I knew I wanted to race. That was the first day of the rest of my life and also the day I got my first ticket and the first time I got my car taken away from me but it wouldn't be the last. I had gotten bit by the speed bug and I quickly discovered a world of racing and knew that I wanted to be a part of it. These kids behind me and any other kid that takes this track might end up with the same need for speed that I did all those years ago. This could be the first day of the rest of their lives. This could be the moment that changes everything for them and I hope it does." My heart slams violently in my chest as the crowd roars with applause. We step forward and cut the red ribbon that is entwined with the black and white checkered ribbon.

Afterwards, we make our way to the stands of the Go-Kart Indy race track and take our seats as the kids climb into the Go-Karts. The go-karts look just like an Indy race car but my mind is lost in the man sitting next to me. He's so much more than I thought he was and it scares me. The Go-Karts come to life and the announcer's voice bellows through the stadium speakers. A green flag is waved and the kids take off. Rathe catches my eye and winks at me. My heart beats a mile a minute. The race is over too soon and if I'm being honest, I didn't see much of it. My mind is running in circles.

Rathe and I are ushered down to the track where the kids are standing. We sign more autographs, take pictures and hang out with mini drivers. One little girl named Luna hasn't left my side. She's adorable and it warms my heart that I can help inspire someone like her. Once her parents come to take her, I scan the crowd to find Jowanna or Rathe. I hear laughter fill the air when I turn around. I see Rathe spinning two little boys around while they laugh with delight. The scene before me makes my heart stop before kick starting again. I realize that I'm falling hard and fast for Rathe McCall and I'm not sure what to do about it.

Thirty-Four

Rathe

Watching Sutton with the kids was an experience. She can be so cold and distant at times I guess I expected her to be that way with them. Instead, she was warm and caring, laughing at their jokes and smiling the whole time. She got down on their level every chance she could. I also noticed the moment her feet started to bother her. There were only a few kids left on the track so I made my way over to Sutton. "Are your feet surviving?"

"Barely," she groans out.

I look her up and down, unable to control myself. "We're almost done here."

"Thank goodness, even though I hate to say that. I had so much fun with these kids today. This has been one of my favorite stops so far," she admits.

Her stormy blue gray eyes seem more blue than gray today. A large, genuine smile graces her face as she looks up at me. "Then you'll love the very last stop where we team up with CD Enterprises."

"Colton Donavan right?"

I nod my head. "Yeah, his wife Rylee is involved with Corporate Cares. It's a place where they deal with orphaned boys. I think they're trying to enlarge the company so they can include girls now too but I'm not sure. Anyways, instead of shuffling kids from foster home to foster home, they place them in one house with a set of counselors that rotate in. They get stability." I don't know why but I can feel the sudden change in Sutton's demeanor. She goes completely still and quiet. I'm just about to ask her if she's okay but Jowanna walks over and announces it's time to wrap things up. I keep a close eye on Sutton. She smiles and laughs with the kids as we prepare to leave but it never looks as genuine as it did earlier. It never seems to reach her eyes. The car ride back to the hotel is quiet and even though Sutton and I are acting as if nothing has changed, I can feel the distance between us. She's withdrawn.

The silence continues as she reaches her door. Sutton looks back over her shoulder at me. "I'm beat. I'm just going to shower and then crawl into bed but I'll see you tomorrow?"

"Yeah, I don't think you get much choice in the matter," I try and joke with her. She smiles but again I notice it's not a true Sutton smile. She opens her door and disappears behind it. I stand there for a while just staring at the closed door trying to figure out what could have caused the shift but I'm coming up with nothing. As I finally give up and step into my room, I can't ignore that pit in my stomach. I know something is bothering Sutton but I don't know her well enough to know how to help her with it. As I pass the adjoining door of our rooms I'm tempted to knock and pull her into my arms. My mom always says that hugs are the best medicine. I used to think it was bullshit but maybe it could help Sutton. However, when I step towards the door and raise my hand to knock, I freeze. She clearly wanted to be alone otherwise she would have asked me to come over, right?

I sigh and step away from the door. Once I reach the bathroom, I turn the shower on as hot as it will go and stand under the heavy stream of scalding hot water until my skin goes numb. Inside the confines of the shower I forget about the world outside. I can forget about racing and rather I'm going to win or lose. There is no worry of anxiety. However, there is Sutton and this nagging feeling in my stomach telling me she just needs someone to hold her and tell her everything is going to be alright.

She's never striked me as that type of woman before but something about that look in her eyes tonight did. In here, though, I can't ignore those growing feelings for her. The ones that are growing too fast, like wildfire in dry woods. She's consuming me in ways I never thought were possible. It's frightening to be honest but at the same time I don't want to fight it. She calms that war of anxiety within me in a way no medicine has ever managed before.

Eventually, the water turns cold and I climb out of the shower, wrapping a towel around my waist. I stop by the fogged mirror and wipe it away so that I can move my hair out of my face. As I enter the bedroom area my eyes are instantly drawn to the form curled up like a ball in the middle of my bed. Her dark hair is damp and covering one of the pillowcases. I make my way to my luggage to pull on some shorts, assuming she's asleep however as I'm quietly rummaging through my suitcase, I feel her arms come around me from behind. She wraps them around my torso with more strength than I could have anticipated. I feel her rest her forehead against the center of my back, her long eyelashes brush lightly against my skin before I feel the light pressure of her feather soft kisses. "You smell good," she says quietly.

"You smell better," I counter. Pulling her hand into mine I bring it up to my nose and inhale the tropical scent that seems to alway cling to her skin before pressing a light kiss to the inside of her wrist. Her pulse beats beneath my lips.

I don't know how long we stand like this but Sutton finally says, "I'm sorry for earlier. I just kind of slipped into my own mind for a bit.

"Was it something I said?"

I can feel Sutton shaking her head no. "It wasn't you. It's just how I'm wired. My head can be a dangerous place sometimes."

"We all have that problem," I tell her. My mind instantly goes to that anxiety that has caused me so many issues lately, especially on the track. I turn around in her arms to face her. I cup her face between my hands and relish how good she feels against me. How is it possible for someone I barely know to feel so right? "Do you want to talk about it?"

She shakes her head slightly as she leans into one of my hands. "No, I just want to be here...with you." Her voice is quiet with her admission.

"That's totally good with me but first I have one question." Sutton raises her eyebrows at me. I can see worry swimming in the pools of her eyes. "How'd you get into my room?" I ask with a laugh.

"I may have told a little white lie to the front desk about getting locked out of my room and when she told me this wasn't my room number I told her we had switched because my bed seemed better for you back." She gives me a mischievous smile and a shrug of her shoulders.

I don't even try to fight off the smirk. "It almost sounds like you're implying that I'm old with back issues."

She pretends to be innocent and all it does is make me want to kiss the hell out of her sharp tongued mouth. "I would never do such a thing but if she came to that conclusion on her own, I can't help it."

I shake my head. "Oh really now?" I tell her as I lean down and scoop her up and over my shoulder. She squeals in surprise as I bring my hand down on her ass before dropping her onto the bed. "I may just have to teach you a lesson."

Sutton gives me a coy smile. "Looks like that was already your plan." She glances down and I realize I lost my towel along the way.

I shrug and meet her eyes. "It would seem like it. Now, let's take your mind off whatever is weighing on it."

She sits up and looks at me. Her eyes are so unguarded right now that it throws me for a loop. "Thank you Rathe."

"You don't need to thank me." I lean down and claim her mouth in a soft kiss that quickly turns into a heated war between us.

Thirty-Five

Sutton

I've never wanted to be open to someone as badly as I do with Rathe. I don't even have a good reason why I want to. There's just something about him that makes me comfortable. Those walls I've built so high to keep everyone out start to crumble when I'm around him. This past week has been eye opening but it's also been a bit scary. I mean sneaking around isn't necessarily the easiest thing. I'm always worried about getting caught especially with Jowanna around. We've been lucky so far because we've been next door to each other in every hotel and they've all had connecting doors. Tonight is the last night of the press tour. We'll be back in California in the morning and the following day is the last event. It's the one for Corporate Cares, the one I'm most curious about. Then the race season will be upon us and who knows what will happen then.

I roll over carefully. I don't want to jostle Rathe's arm that is resting on my body. I like to watch him while he's sleeping. His face is so stress free, the worry line between his eyebrows is missing and I swear there's a little smile constantly on his face. I reach out and gently trace the outline of his lips. I'm worried about what will happen when this tour is over. What becomes of us? I mean did this only start because we've been pushed together every day and right next door to one another every night? Was it out of convenience and loneliness? I know my answer and it terrifies me but I need to know his.

Rathe stirs slightly and I jerk my fingertip away from his lips. "Mmm...don't stop doing that it feels nice." His voice is thick with sleep.

"I didn't mean to wake you," I whisper. I don't know why I'm whispering except that in the quiet of his room it feels like that's how things should be said. I don't want to disturb the peaceful bubble we've found.

Rathe shakes his head slightly. "You didn't. I was awake before you turned over. I was going to tell you but then you started tracing my lips and it felt so good."

I chuckle. "I'm glad you didn't find it weird."

Rathe's chocolate brown eyes find mine. Even though I can't see in the dark, I can feel them on me. "I don't find a single thing about you weird, Sutton. Intriguing...yes, but weird...definitely not."

The silence falls between us, it's not awkward, just heavy. I feel like we are both holding back. I know my reasons but I'm curious what his reasons are. "So, are you ready to get back home?"

Rathe shrugs. "As ready as you can be. I mean I don't know what I'm ready for to be honest. The quicker we get home the closer we are to race season and I don't know what will happen when I'm on the track in an actual race. It's scary."

"I think you're going to do great. There's this feeling in my gut telling me that you are going to own that track this season."

He scoots forward and lightly presses his lips to mine. "Thank you. I mean obviously we don't know how I'll react in a real race. I could completely freeze up again but I needed to hear that."

"Then I'm glad I could help." Rathe tightens his grip on me and pulls me closer. I snuggle into his chest breathing in the scent of his soap, clean and masculine as my eyes drift closed. A few hours later I wake up to the sound of Rathe rummaging around the room. I sit up in the bed. "Is everything okay?"

He turns around, his face in a full smile and his eyes light with life. "It's great." He walks over to the bed and leans down before claiming my mouth as his. "Good morning beautiful."

I don't even attempt to fight the smile that graces my face. "Good morning. You're in a really good mood."

"I am. So, I'm assuming you're free tonight." Rathe watches me with eager eyes.

I laugh. "Yeah, I think it's safe to say that. The only plans I have had during this press tour have been with you and the bed."

Rathe bites down on his lower lip. "And I love those plans but I made us some different plans for tonight."

"What? Why?" The worry and unease is instant in my gut. It's the tone of his voice when he says plans that has me worried.

"We're going to go out," he announces.

I shake my head, quickly dismissing the idea. "Rathe, we can't go out."

"Why not?" he asks.

My eyes bug out of their sockets. I'm actually shocked they didn't pop out and roll across the bed. "The contract for starters. Oh and we aren't supposed to like each other."

Rathe holds up a hand to stop me. "Technically, it never said we couldn't *like* each other. The two of us hanging out doesn't break the contract in any way."

"I don't know…"

"Sutton, I'm sure they'd like us to at least seem like friends. They don't have to know what goes on between us outside of that. The plans I made will just look friendly to anyone outside of us. They'll never know the difference. I'd never jeopardize your career but I do think it would be good for both of us to have some time with one another outside of the four walls of a hotel room." Rathe looks at me expectantly.

The look on his face and my own ridiculous hope has me actually considering this idea. I always believed hope was a dangerous thing and I've fought with my own negativity. When you're thrown into the system you learned not to hope for much in the world but right now, I can't win the battle within my body. Eventually, I sigh and tell him, "Okay, we can play nice and friendly for them. A night out that has nothing to do with the tour will be nice."

Rathe claps his hands and his grin grows ten times larger. I didn't even think that would be possible. "You won't regret it." That pit in my stomach tells me I will but I ignore it anyways.

Thirty-Six

Sutton

I'm not sure what to expect tonight. I didn't exactly pack for a date in mind. Actually, this isn't a date. It's just two teammates going out together to relieve the stress of a press tour. I have to keep reminding myself of that so I don't cross a line or make things awkward. The pounding of my heart keeps reminding me that I've already crossed so many lines. I never intended for any of this yet here I am. Rathe wouldn't tell me what he had planned for us despite my begging but he did tell me I could dress comfortably so I decided on a pair of red denim shorts and a loose fitting black tank top with my signature Converse of course. I let my hair do whatever it naturally does because with this humidity there's no point in fighting it. My makeup is light as well. There's a knock on the door and instantly a swarm of pigeons takes up home in my stomach. I open the door and Rathe is standing there looking like he just walked out of a movie. His hair is perfectly messy, beard trimmed to perfection, clothes simple and comfortable which instantly makes me feel better about what I picked out to wear. His heated eyes roam my body from head to toe and the pigeons in my stomach morph into a raging wildfire. "Damn, I wish I could step into your space right now and devour that look in your eyes…" The look in his eyes tells me he's being honest. The wild fire turns into a full blown inferno at that confession. "But considering all the people in the hallway currently I better exercise my self-control." I laugh and he shakes his head. "I'm serious woman. You look amazing."

I feel the flush coating my body along with the goosebumps racing over my skin. "Thanks." I grab my purse and make sure my room key is tucked inside. "So, you want to tell me what we're doing now?"

Rathe chuckles. "You either aren't good with someone else being in control or you don't like surprises."

"Both," I answer without a second thought.

Rathe studies me as we make our way to the elevator bay. "Noted but I can promise you're going to have a ton of fun."

"Didn't someone tell you that you shouldn't make promises you can't keep."

The elevator doors open, it's empty as we step inside. I feel Rathe on my heels, his body heat wrapping around me like a blanket. When he leans down his breath tickles the skin on the back of my neck. "Oh, I keep my promises Sutton."

I don't reply because honestly what could I say to that? I want him to keep his promises to me but I know better than to actually believe in something like that. Even a person with the best intentions will fail at keeping a promise. The world will change and the people in it change as well. Promises are changed or broken, it's just the way of the world. When we step outside of the hotel the valet steps forward and hands a set of keys to Rathe. A beautiful burnt orange Astin Martin DB2 is sitting in front of me. A true classic car. It causes my heart to race. It's a truly beautiful piece of art. "Wow," I whisper. I'm afraid if I say it any louder that I'll break the magic of the moment.

"That fact that you can appreciate the true beauty of this car only makes you more beautiful." Rathe steps forward and opens the passenger side door for me.

I look up at his dark eyes. "Is it yours?"

"It is as of a couple hours ago." Rathe smirks before he shuts the door and walks around to the driver's side of the car. The car is a convertible and the top is already down so I grab a hair tie from my bag and quickly pull my hair into a messy bun. "You ready for a night you won't be able to forget?" He wags his eyebrows at me and I can't help but laugh at how silly he looks.

Rathe drives us through downtown Miami. It's a beautiful city with tons of culture. You can hear the Latin music coming from inside some of the buildings we're passing. The air is filled with the smell of Cuban food and the underlying sea salt from the ocean. Rathe pulls in front of the tallest building I've seen here yet and hops out. He hands his keys to the valet before turning towards me and opening the car door. Rathe extends his hand to help me out. I'm reluctant at first to take it because what if someone sees? We could be jeopardizing everything. However, one look into those eyes so full of hope and mischief and I know it'll be worth it. When my skin comes into contact with his, the fire reignites within me, so strong even the ocean a few blocks away couldn't put it out. "What are we doing here?" I hear screaming coming from above us but I can't make much out right now.

"Trust me," Rathe tells me as he places his hand on the small of my back and leads us inside. I don't really have time to take in our surroundings because Rathe waves at a young man standing at a podium to greet us. I believe we are at a hotel or maybe a club of some sort but I never see behind the large wooden doors. Rathe ushers us towards the elevator which we take to the top floor. He looks down at my shoes. "I'm glad you wore those shoes because we have to climb the last flight of stairs."

I'm half excited, half worried about what I'm going to be walking into but I follow behind Rathe quietly. Every now and then he glances back over his shoulder in my direction to check on me. Eventually, we reach the top and knock on the door. A young girl opens it and Rathe gives her his undercover name in an attempt to secure our privacy. As I step through the door I hear a squeal and look to my right where I see a zipline set up. I swing my head back to Rathe. "We're ziplining?"

"Technically, we're going to eat."

I scoff. "Oh really? Where? The moon?"

Rathe laughs. "No, just over there," he tells me pointing. I follow the direction he's pointing and see another building a couple of blocks away that is slightly shorter than the one we're currently standing on. I can't make anything out from here though. Rathe urges me into the line of people waiting to zipline next. From here the city looks gorgeous but I always had a thing for city lights. Rathe leans down. "Are you okay?" I just nod my head in reply. "You aren't afraid of heights, are you?"

"Kind of. I mean I've never really been this high up until now. I'm not sure what to think." I hate admitting that since it probably makes me seem so inexperienced compared to him but it's the truth. Rathe and I come from completely different worlds. This is yet another reminder of that but I won't let that damper the evening or my mood. Before I know it I step up and get harnessed into the zipline. When I look down at the city below me, I get a little dizzy. "I'm not sure I can do this."

I feel his presence behind me before I feel the warmth of his hand on my shoulder. "You've got this."

I nod my head. "So, what was the point of this again? I mean what's on the other side of this zipline that was so important that we just had to go this route?"

"Dinner," he replies simply before the employee pushes me away from the building.

I scream at first but it quickly morphs. The wind whips through my hair. It reminds me of being in my car, racing. Adrenaline quickly takes over my body and I let myself enjoy the moment, to drink in the city in a way most people will never do. The city lights are a beautiful blur and Rathe was right, this is a night I'll always remember.

Thirty-Seven

Rathe

This zip line and rooftop dinner has been on my bucket list since I first visited Miami a few years ago. I never had time in my schedule to do it though, until now. The fact that I brought Sutton with me says a lot but there is this part of me that doesn't want to acknowledge how my feelings for her have grown over these two weeks. It seems like such a small, insignificant amount of time but for me it's changed just about everything.

I watch as the employee pushes Sutton away from the ledge. The initial squeal, partial scream that comes from her causes me to laugh but I can tell the moment she actually starts to enjoy it. I'm really glad I brought her with me to experience this. I hadn't considered that she might be scared of heights until we were already on the roof. I just figured this was something that would be right up her alley. She seems like a bit of an adrenaline monkey, much like myself.

"Your turn sir," the employee that just pushed Sutton away from the building tells me. I step up and let them adjust my harness and connect me to the zip line. Standing on the ledge of the building, looking down at the world below, well it's frightening really. I didn't expect to have such a nervous flutter racing through my body. Heights have never bothered me but this right now, is testing me. "Are you ready?"

I nod my head. "Yeah, let's do it," I reply. Taking the first step off the ledge was the worst. There's a split second where you are in free fall before the harness snatches you and sends you speeding through two blocks of the city, high above the streets and pedestrians. The city lights are a blur as you whirl past them but it's a total rush. The zip line starts to slow as I approach the rooftop of the destination. I spot Sutton standing to the side, a smile from ear to ear on her face. She looks slightly wind blown but so damn beautiful that my chest aches. The employees pull me in and get me unhooked. Once the harness is removed, I step down. "So, how was that?"

She gives me a coy smile before rolling her eyes. "As much as I hate to admit it, that was definitely something I'll never forget."

I pump my fist in the air like I just won something huge. "Yes! I knew it!"

"How did you find out about all of this anyways?" Sutton asks.

The hostess greets us before leading us to a table near the edge of the roof. The lighting is muted, just a soft, warm glow. The iron table with glass tops are just enough for two people. A small vase with two yellow flowers sit in the middle along with a candle lit lantern. The entire rooftop is done to make you feel like you are in another place and up here, above the city, it's easy to slip into that feeling. Everything feels very romantic. Sutton sits across from me and studies the menu. "To answer your question, this is something that's been on my bucket list. I found out about it a few years ago when I first visited Miami but I've never had enough time to do it. Miami is usually in the middle of the press tour, not at the end. We lucked out this time."

"Seems like it. That was amazing." Her eyes roam as they take in the city around us. I wish I could see everything for her eyes. I wish I could hear what she is thinking.

I smile over at her. "I'm glad you enjoyed it."

Sutton nods her head and takes in our surroundings once more. "This place is really beautiful too. It almost has a Moroccan vibe to it."

"It's gorgeous," I tell her but my eyes haven't left her face. I don't know what's happening to me. I've never been that guy. The one who has lines or plans big dates. This isn't something I'm used to but I just wanted this time away with her. Away from the spotlight, racing and our contracts. Somewhere we can just be Rathe and Sutton without all the complications sitting on our shoulders at the moment.

The waiter comes and goes, he takes our orders, brings our drinks and food all the while Sutton and I just talk. I feel the slow shift within my body. That same magnetic pull to her that I felt the first day at the track, when she took her helmet off. I want to know more about her. I want to know everything but she's got a wall of defense I need to take down first. It won't be an easy task but I'm not one for giving up. "So, tell me about yourself?"

Sutton's fork freezes midair. I almost feel like I asked her to solve a physics equation. "There's not much to say. I'm not close to any of my biological family so Evanna is my family. We've had each other's backs through everything."

"Sounds like Ryann, Maxton and I."

She nods her head. "Exactly like that." Silence falls between us but there's something uneasy about it now. I can't pinpoint it but it's there. Sutton looks around the city. "I always love city lights but I never thought I'd witness them like this. This has to be my favorite part about tonight."

"Why city lights?" I ask. Curiosity getting the best of me. I don't miss how she averts her gaze to her plate, refusing to look up and meet my eyes. Her shoulders dip ever so slightly. I want to know why but something tells me that even if she explains why she likes city lights I still won't know why she seems so alone sometimes.

Sutton shrugs. "I don't know exactly. They were always beautiful, always consistent. As long as there is electricity there will be city lights. They keep the world from getting too scary. I mean look around. If the city was pitch black right now it'd be frightening but with the lights, it's beautiful and hopeful. When you grow up in the sketchy part of town you look for hope even if you find it hard to believe in, beauty and consistency wherever you can find it."

Her words are beautiful, she's beautiful. I want to tell her that but the question falls from my tongue quicker. I didn't want to ask her because she'll probably close down the minute that I ask. "Sketchy part of town?"

"Yeah, not all of us grow up princesses." Silence falls between us and I know that's all I'm going to get from her. I want to know so much more. There's this burning need to know it all but I know I can't push her and I'm not even sure I should push myself right now.

Eventually, we fall into our easy banter as we eat. I watch as the muted lighting casts a golden halo over her face. Her eyes almost look solid blue in this light but I miss the stormy gray added to the blue depths I've come accustomed to. Once we finish eating, we take the elevator down to the bottom of the building. "Do you feel like a little walk before we grab the car?"

"Sure," she replies with a bright smile. I'm glad she seems to be the Sutton that I know again. I've learned there's two versions of her. The first version is the one I know, the one most people know. It's the one she allows people to see. She smiles and acts a certain way that is not always her. The other version is the one that seems lonely, holding on to secrets that weigh her down when she could share that burden with those who care about her. I want to know both but I'm scared of the other version. I've never been the best at being there for someone else. What if I can't be what she needs when I ask for that version?

I lead us a few blocks away. We pass live musicians playing for tips and fun. People dancing. Cafes and boutiques, clubs and bars and more than enough people before we finally reach the beach. "You like the city lights and I like the beach at night, without all the hustle and bustle of the crowds of people. I like the peaceful quiet and solitude of the beach at night."

Sutton wraps her arms around herself. "It almost seems like you're all alone."

"Yeah, I guess sometimes it does. In my world being alone isn't the worst thing to happen to me. I rarely get a moment alone during race season. You'll see what I mean soon enough." I scan the area to make sure we're alone before I step forward and pull her into me. I breathe in her scent that calms the anxiety that lives in my blood. Leaning down I take her mouth as if it's the lifeline I need and maybe it is.

Thirty-Eight

Sutton

Being back in my own bed in Sunnyville feels odd after two weeks of sleeping in hotels next to Rathe. My bed now feels empty and cold. I roll over and reach to the other side as if that can magically summon his body next to mine. It's early and I should be jet lagged but I'm wide awake. Technically today is the last day of our press tour. There is a full day function for Corporate Cares sponsored by CD Enterprises and then a banquet tonight. This is the only function I've been looking forward to on the entire schedule. Maybe I'm biased because it's a matter that hits so close to home for me.

I climb out of my bed and head into the kitchen to grab a soda. I need the caffeine. After raiding the fridge and eating more than my share of junk food I camp out on the couch to watch Clueless. Evanna stumbles in about halfway through the movie and tosses herself down next to me. "I can't believe you're watching Clueless without me, you bitch."

I laugh. "Wow, such a warm welcome after my absence. I guess that saying about the 'absence making the heart grow fonder' isn't true after all."

Evanna gives me a glare. "I still love you but you know Christian is my man. He's so dreamy." Evanna literally sighs like some school girl.

My eyes roll on their own accord. "No, definitely not. I think you need to go find those glasses you refuse to wear because it's all about Josh."

"Josh?" Evanna scoffs. "The tree hugging, step brother?"

"Dude, it's Paul Rudd. He's like forty and still looks too damn good. Besides, he was the best guy in the movie."

Evanna shakes her head and makes a gagging noise. "Now, I think you're the one that needs glasses."

"Whatever," I counter back at her.

Evanna gives me her best sneer. "As if." For a moment we just stare one another down before we cave and crack up. Evanna launches herself into my arms. "I missed you! This house was so quiet while you were gone. I even considered throwing raging parties every night."

"You did not but I missed you too!" I hug her back. Evanna and I have had the same argument over Christian and Josh from Clueless for years. Every time we watch the movie, we know that it's coming. "So, tell me what I missed here?"

Evanna shakes her head. "Oh no you don't. You are not going to come back and dodge the Rathe subject. You're the one that has details to spill, not me, so get to spilling sister."

I shrug and avoid her eye contact. "There's not really anything to tell. I mean I'm sure you watched most of the videos and clips from the tour online or over social media."

"I'm not talking about the damn tour! I'm talking about you sleeping next door to Rathe McCall and this weird attraction the two of you share but fight as if it's the worst idea ever." Evanna huffs and I can't help but laugh. She's being slightly dramatic but she has no idea how close to the truth she is.

"You have no idea how bad of an idea Rathe and I are," I admit to her quietly.

"What do you mean?" Evanna sits up. That's the thing about her. She knows when to give you hell, when to make you laugh, when to be your shoulder to cry on, and when to be your ear to listen. She's the best friend anyone could ask for.

My head falls back to rest on the couch and I roll it towards her. The truth is on the tip of my tongue and I know if I can trust anyone with this truth it's her but it almost feels like if I say it out loud I'm setting myself up to get hurt which is ridiculous because I'm already there. "These two weeks have been so confusing Evanna. I mean at first Rathe was hot and cold again and it was frustrating. I basically was ready to give up but then Rathe kissed me and I swear I melted like a popsicle on a hot summer day."

"That good huh?" Evanna asks, eyebrows raised.

The memory comes rushing back. "I felt it everywhere, from the top of my head to the tip of my toes." Evanna lets out a low whistle while fanning herself dramatically. "Then things basically went cold again."

"What the actual hell?" she asks.

"Well, it turns out we literally can't have a relationship because of a clause in our contract but then we spent the better half of our tour sneaking around at night. I think we even had a date last night in Miami." Last night has been on replay since it happened. I can't shake the feelings I have for Rathe or the way he's taking down my walls, one brick at a time. Evanna asks for details and I gladly fill her in because I need to tell someone. I also need someone to tell me I'm not crazy for risking everything over Rathe and whatever might be between us.

Evanna sits back on the couch after I'm finished recapping the last two weeks. "Wow, I don't even know what to say. I'm shocked and so damn proud at the same time. I mean Ryann and I knew there was something between the two of you but we had no idea it was this hot."

I shake my head. "It doesn't matter how hot it is, Evanna. It's breaking the rules of our contracts. It'd be crazy to risk our careers for whatever is between us, right?"

She sighs. "You know me Sutton. I'm a hopeless romantic. That part of me is dominant, so yes, I'd risk a career that I barely started for love. I'd do it without a second thought but you're not me Sutton. You've always wanted security and I can't fault you for that. Especially given our childhood. So, do what makes you happy, that's the best advice I have for you."

Of course Evanna would choose Rathe over racing. It'd be an easy decision for her but she's right, I don't think the same way she does. I'd choose my career because it's what will keep me above water and give my life meaning, long after he's gone. I sigh. "Will come with me today?"

"You know I will."

I stand up. "Great, let's go get dressed then." I stand in front of my closet for too long, debating on what to wear. Finally, I remind myself that I'm still the same Sutton and I need to put on what I'm comfortable in. I grab a pair of black denim cutoffs, a distressed Guns n' Roses t-shirt that shows just enough skin to be cool and sexy and toss on my black Converse. I have Evanna French braid the scalp of my hair and pull the rest into a messy bun. I go light on the makeup since we're going to be outside for most of the day anyways. I throw on a pair of earrings I bought from Jowanna that she had made on a whim during the tour that match my shirt and grab my sunglasses.

When I step out of my room Evanna's mouth falls open. "Okay, where's Sutton?"

I roll my eyes. "You're being ridiculous."

She shakes her head. "No, I'm not. You look hot and Rathe isn't going to know what hit him when we get there."

"It doesn't matter. We can't be together in public so none of this matters but if we're late it does, so let's go." I tell her as I slip my sunshades into place and head out to my car. Evanna is quiet on the drive over to the racetrack for CD Enterprises. I know she has a ton of shit she wants to say and she's biting her tongue because right now I need to plaster on my public smile and do my job. I'm grateful for that right now. As we pull up I find the parking lot of the race track completely packed. I grab the first spot I can find. Evanna whimpers next to me and I look down to see her feet in a pair of wedges. "Oh hell, you really should have worn a different pair of shoes."

"Shut up! I wasn't expecting to have to walk this far," she says as she climbs out of the car.

I laugh. "Even if we weren't walking this far you're going to be standing and walking around the majority of the day."

"Well, it's not like Converse go with this outfit," she tells me as she spins around in her sundress.

"We'll see how you feel about Converse in a bit. Let's go fashionista." My nerves grow with each step we take. While I was getting ready to come here, I had scanned my phone and seen some missed texts from Rathe but I read them but never replied because I'm not sure what to do about him. Now, I'm worried about how he's going to act in person. Maybe, I should have at least answered him back but it's too late to worry about that now. We're halfway through the parking lot when I hear his laughter and when I turn to find him I see him walking with a tall, willowy redhead that makes my skin crawl. My stomach churns and despite the sunglasses he's wearing I know the moment his eyes land on me. His entire body goes rigid.

"Oh shit," Evanna says next to me.

I shake my head and grab her hand. "Come on, let's go."

Thirty-Nine

Rathe

Last night was rough. I missed having Sutton beside me. I missed her warmth and soft snores that sometimes sound like little hums. I miss her scent clinging to the pillows and invading my senses. The first thing I wanted to do this morning was text her but I fought that need off. I didn't want to seem too clingy but then when I finally did text her, she never replied. Her silence almost made me feel like the last two weeks never happened. So, when my agent said he lined me up a "date" which is his fancy term for someone that he lines up for me to appear with at events, I was reluctant to agree but couldn't say now. It's mutually beneficial for the both of us and usually our agents are friends so they like to help one another out. Normally, having a date to one of these things doesn't bother me but today it felt wrong. I kept checking my phone up until I actually left to pick up Tabitha, an upcoming runway model, but there was never any reply to my texts. My ego and pride were bruised and I let that guide my judgement.

However, when I looked up and saw Sutton standing there it felt like the world literally stopped moving. I didn't need to see her eyes behind her shades to know the moment she saw Tabitha and I. Her heated glare was on me and there was a falter in her armor. It was barely noticeable but it was there. The moment when her face fell, I knew I royally screwed up. As quickly as that moment came, it went, replaced with the version of Sutton that doesn't let people in. I saw her walls that I had been working to take down, go back up, higher and stronger than ever.

I couldn't even meet Evanna's gaze because I knew I'd see disappointment. Ryann had already mentioned that Evanna and her thought I had feelings for Sutton and with Evanna being Sutton's best friend I'm sure she knows what happened over these past two weeks. Then again maybe she doesn't. Maybe, I'm Sutton's dirty little secret. Maybe, she regrets it all now that we're back on our territory. Just because I fell for her in the matter of fourteen days doesn't mean she fell for me. There's a good chance that I've misread this whole situation. Tabitha and I continue towards the racetrack where there are all kinds of things set up. There's food being cooked, face painting, games and tons of racers for the kids to mingle with. However, I barely register any of this or what Tabitha is saying because my mind is trying to piece together Sutton and whatever the hell is going on with us.

"Earth to Rathe," Ryann says, waving her hand in my face.

I shake my head and tuck away my thoughts and feelings for Sutton away. "Hey, sorry I was a little zoned out."

"Yeah, I caught that. I also caught that you brought another damn girl with you. What the hell dude?" Ryann places her hands on her hips. It's the stance that lets everyone know she means business.

I sigh and rub at the back of my neck. "Tabitha, go on ahead and check the stuff out." She nods and makes her way through the crowd. I wait until she's gone before I turn back to my sister. "Not that it is any of your business but I'm not really with her. Kevin, my agent if you can remember, likes to set up these "dates" that are mutually beneficial for us. That's all this is but last time I checked I didn't owe anything to anyone."

"That's bullshit and you know it."

"Is it?" I ask, my eyebrows raising with the question.

Ryann scoffs and shakes her head. "Why are you so damn stubborn? You have feelings for Sutton, I know it."

A few of the people standing just a few feet away from us turn to look and I curse under my breath. I grab my sister's arm and pull her back into the tunnel that leads out of the racetrack. "Will you keep it down?"

"Rathe, what's going on? Seriously? I mean Sutton is great. She's beautiful, helping you get over your fear of really letting go while racing again. I know you like her and I'm pretty damn sure she likes you but then you show up with the wannabe Barbie which is confusing." I can see Ryann trying to figure out what's going on and I know I might as well tell her because if I don't, she'll just pester me until I do.

"Look, I like her. We had a great time while on the tour and I think she's amazing but it'll never work. We can't be together."

Ryann laughs. "You're being a little dramatic, don't you think? I thought that was normally my role."

"I'm not being dramatic Ryann. We literally can't be together because it's in our damn contracts." I explain everything to her and I watch as her face grows sad.

She sighs. "This sucks. I was rooting for the two of you."

"Yeah, well even if the contract wasn't a factor, I don't think she roots for the two of us." I look out and see her standing with Evanna and some of the kids from the Corporate Cares program. Before Ryann can start in I tell her, "We should get back out there." I lead the way. I busy myself throughout the first part of the day and by busy myself I mean avoid Sutton. I'm thinking I can keep it up until I end up talking to Colton. We may be big rivals on the track but I have mad respect for him as a person. He clearly loves his wife and does everything he can to help raise money for the program where she works. Colton and I are talking when Rylee, Colton's wife, and Sutton approaches us.

"I'm sorry to interrupt but I was just talking to Sutton and she brought up a great point. Why doesn't Corporate Cares expand over to include orphaned girls as well as orphaned boys? I mean I know I discussed it with Teddy when I first started working with Corporate Cares and again recently but just trying to get the funding for the boys was a struggle so we put it back on the shelf again. Sutton reminded me of why it was so important to have a stable environment for the girls as well." Rylee's face is flushed with excitement but when I brave a glance at Sutton, I see nothing but uncertainty.

"Sounds like this is something that you're passionate about Sutton. I mean my wife doesn't get this excited over just anything," Colton tells her.

Sutton plasters on her fake smile. It's scary that I can actually distinguish which smile is real or fake. "I just know from personal experience that having a stable living environment like the ones being provided to these boys would have meant the world to me. Granted I wouldn't have met my best friend if I hadn't been shuffled from foster home to foster home...but the idea of actually having a place to call home and people to rely on. That's every child's dream."

My heart stops. Sutton was in the system? I'm an ass. Things start to make sense. Her wall of defense, the loneliness I see in her eyes sometimes and the way she spent so little of the money she got for signing the contract. Yes, she bought a house and a car for herself and one for Evanna but she bought a house and cars that just about any working class person can afford. For her that's all she needs because it's a safe place. I want to reach out and pull her into me but I know I can't. At least, not here, right now and that makes me so mad. This whole time I thought she was some spoiled, rich princess but it turns out she couldn't be farther from it.

"You know maybe CD Enterprises and Revv-It Racing could work together during this race season to help secure the funding to add the girl's home to the Corporate Cares agenda." Colton smiles as his thoughts unfold.

I clear my throat and manage to tear my eyes back away from Sutton. "I'd like to help with that. I think that's a great cause."

"Hell yeah, man. I'm glad to hear it." Colton and Rylee start brainstorming ideas but it's Suttons eyes I feel on me. When I brave a look at her I see so many questions hidden in those pools of blue gray. I can't read all of hers but I hope she can read mine. It's my apology and my promise to make it up to her. It's letting her know that I want nothing more than to hold her right now even though I can't. It's me telling her that I'm falling for her...hard and fast and I can't stop it even if I wanted to. We're racing on this track now, just the two of us.

Forty

Sutton

Somehow, I managed to get out of a full day on the track with Corporate Cares. I hadn't expected Rylee to be so excited about my question concerning female orphans. I also hadn't expected her to run right over to her husband who was talking to Rathe so she could discuss it with him. A part of me loves the fact that she loved the idea, wants to pitch to the main guy in charge and even has my input on certain things. Another part of me is mentally beating myself up because I don't know why I even brought it up. It's not like I walk around telling people about my past. There's actually very few people that know I was in the foster care system.

I sigh as I examine myself in the mirror. Tonight is the charity gala for the Corporate Cares and CD Enterprises. It's formal so a gown and heels were necessary but a large part of me wishes I could just skip this all together. I mean it's going to be hard to avoid Rathe and talking about my past with tons of potential donors for the foundation. I already know that my story is going to become the platform that Corporate Cares uses to help launch the female orphan homes. I'm glad I can help and possibly make a difference for some other girl who finds herself in a situation similar to mine but it doesn't make me any more comfortable. I also don't want a bunch of fake pity for how my life was growing up. I've let go of my past the best I can and moved forward and I don't want to dwell on it now nor do I want anyone else to. I've seen enough of those fake saddened eyes to last me a lifetime.

Evanna appears in the door. "You look amazing even though I know you aren't feeling it."

"I'm really glad you picked the green," I tell her. Evanna knows today was a rough one for me. She knows that I'm not looking forward to tonight but as always, she's stayed by my side all day. She helped do my makeup and hair and then pick out a gown for me to wear. When she first pulled the form fitting, strapless emerald green gown I cringed. It had ivy like lace over the fitted bodice and flared like a mermaid mid-calf. However, the shock factor is the sheer ivy designed lace covering my sides where the bodice disappears, leaving my skin exposed with just the lace to cover. The dress is sexy without being in your face. As I stand in the mirror and examine all of the hard work that Evanna has put in I can honestly say I feel as if I look the part. For the first time since I signed the contract with Revv-It I feel like I fit into this world. Evanna left my hair down and curled it with a large curling iron, creating perfect waves. My makeup is light with a nude lip but a smokey eye. My dress fits me like a glove and I can feel my inner confidence doing a dance.

"Me too because you rock the shit out of that." Evanna comes into the room and stands behind me. Her caramel colored skin is flawless as usual but it's her honey colored eyes so full of emotion that make it hard for me to breathe for a moment. "I know that this isn't ideal for you. Things with Rathe seem to be one way then another. Now, you're going to have to talk about your childhood and what you experienced in the system and I know it's not a subject you take lightly or like to talk about but I'm so proud of you Sutton. I've always known that you're this amazing, beautiful, talented and caring person. You just have a hard time showing it but now the world is getting a glimpse of her."

I look away, unable to deal with the emotions that her words are creating within me. "You know if you keep this up I'm going to cry and look like a drowned rat by the time I get to the gala and all your hard work will have been for nothing."

Evanna laughs then sniffs. "Oh no, we can't have that." The doorbell echoes throughout the house. "That must be your limo. I'll go grab the door." I watch as Evanna disappears out of my room. I do one more look over to make sure I look my part before grabbing my clutch and heading out to the limo Revv-It Racing has sent over. I grab Evanna in the doorway and hug her goodbye before actually leaving.

The limo ride is quiet and surprisingly quick. When I pull up I'm shocked to see the amount of media in front of the hotel where the gala is being held. I shouldn't be shocked considering that Colton Donavan is often in the media spotlight but somehow, I just didn't think it would follow him into the Corporate Cares world. Seeing all the flashing cameras makes me realize how wrong I was. Nerves hit me full force. All of these people are going to know about my past. They will post about it online as well as in newspapers and magazines. It'll be out there for the world to see. I had been so focused on the possible donors that I didn't consider the rest of the world.

My palms instantly grow clammy and my heart races as if it's on a track. What the hell am I doing here? I don't belong here. You can dress up trash all you want but at the end of the day it's still trash. That's me, I'm the trash. This isn't my world and it never will be, not really anyways. The limo pulls to a stop and the driver gets out to open my door. I take deep breaths in an attempt to calm myself while he's walking around the car but I'm only two breaths in when the door swings open and a hand that I've become all too familiar with appears. I'm frozen in my spot until Rathe leans down and meets my eyes. "You're going to have to get out of the car."

"What are you doing here?" I whisper. I'm not sure how he even hears me over the roar of the media hollering his name, just trying to snap a picture of him.

"Currently, I'm trying to escort you inside the gala."

I shake my head. "What about the contract?"

"Two teammates attending a gala that is linked to another Indy racer doesn't seem to be breaking the contract, does it?" he asks, eyebrows raised. I shake my head. "Then take my hand Sutton."

"Where's the redhead?" I hate how my tone is laced with hurt and jealousy. It's the two things I don't want him to know he caused me.

Rathe shakes his head. "Okay, we're going to do this now." Suddenly, he's climbing through the door and taking a seat beside me. "Driver, can you make a few laps around the block?" The car lurches forward suddenly.

"What the hell are you doing?" I ask. My nerves morph into anger quicker than I expect.

"Explaining." It's his only answer. A part of me wants an explanation but the other part of me doesn't. I fell for Rathe while we were on tour and I'm not sure I can handle another disappointment right now. I turn away from him and look out the window as the city passes us by. I feel his hand encase mine but I quickly and regrettably yank mine away. Instantly, I miss the warmth and comfort of his skin. "This should be fun," he comments quietly. I whip around. He smirks but it falls from his face quickly.

"Save it Rathe. I don't need your excuses or fake apologies. We had a thing out of convenience. We were away from home and lonely and got caught up in the moment. You thought you'd slum it with the poor orphaned girl who was thrust onto your team and into your life. Guess what, the tour is over and so are we." I turn away from him. I can't look at him and hide everything I'm feeling inside. A huge part of me wants him to fight for me but it won't happen. He made it clear this afternoon where I stood with him. Actions always speak louder than words. I should have known he'd never pick me. My own father didn't even care enough to pick me. Why would Rathe? "Driver!" The window between us comes down. "Pull over please."

The driver slows before coming to a stop. I throw the door open and climb out, making sure to lift my dress to keep it from getting dirty. I hear the door before him. "What the hell Sutton?"

I stop on the sidewalk but I don't turn around to face him. "Just save it Rathe. I'm doing us both a favor. I'm doing the one thing you obviously didn't know how to do."

"Sutton, I didn't even know about your past until today so what happened on the press tour had nothing to do with that." I hear the plea in his voice and it pulls on every single thing I feel for him but I choose to ignore it.

I shrug. "Either way we're done. We have an event to attend and I'm sure your date is waiting. I'll see you there."

"You can't just walk there," Rathe calls out to me.

"You can bet your ass I can and if you keep standing there, you can watch me," I call back to him over my shoulder. I have two blocks to get my shit together because if I won't let the world see me fall you can damn well guarantee Rathe McCall won't either.

Forty-One

Rathe

I stand there for who knows how long but long enough that eventually the driver of the limo gets out and comes up to me. I wave him away and eventually I walk the two blocks to the event. I knew things would be different once we got back to Sunnyville but I had no idea they would blow up like this. I had no idea everything would go up in smoke in one day. As I walk, I replay the past two weeks away from everything and try to figure out what happened when we got back home. What happened from the time she got off the plane until this morning? What caused her to not reply to my texts? I understand that seeing me and Tabitha together wasn't ideal but there were a lot of factors. It's not like I could tell Kevin no. If I had he'd want to know who I was taking and I couldn't reply with Sutton's name. Our contracts and that damn clause are the actual issue. It keeps us from just being who we are when we're around each other.

I have to figure out how to fix this. I don't know how but I know there has to be a way. I just need to get her to listen to me. When I reach the event the red carpet is still just as crammed with media as it was when I left. Taking a deep breath I step onto the carpet and prepare for the craziness that always comes along with the media. My name is yelled from every direction, the flashes from the camera are blinding and regardless of how many carpets you walk, camera flashes are never anything you can get used to. I do my best to give them all what they want and need but I know that tomorrow there will be some story about how I stiffed a person. It's frustrating but unfortunately, part of the territory.

Eventually, I make it inside. The room is decorated in red, black and white. It instantly screams a CD Enterprises event but on every table is a picture of the kids that Corporate Cares helps to raise. They also hang on the wall along with achievements that the boys have made since living in the care of the counselors in a stable environment provided by the company that Rylee works for. It's amazing to see. Seeing things like this reminds me that sometimes things do work out. There's still hope in the world and that's okay.

I make my way around the room, taking time to study each picture hanging on the wall. The smiles on the boy's faces draw you in. They all seem so happy and it makes me wonder what Sutton went through. If I had seen her as a child would she have had a smile on her face like this? Or was she just tossed around from place to place, with no one to really care for her, like so many of the system horror stories I've heard about? The idea of her childhood being like that guts me. I scan the room and find her standing with Rylee and Colton as the three of them talk with some older gentleman in his three-thousand-dollar suit and his much younger date. Sutton's smiling now but I know it's not real. It's her act for the benefit of the gala. To help create a safe haven for orphaned girls. I've seen a real Sutton smile and this isn't it.

The moment she steps away from the group I beeline in her direction as she makes her way out of the room. I catch up to her just before she reaches the restroom. When my hand wraps around her elbow, the jolt to my system from the softness of her skin, the familiarity of it, settles upon me. She sighs but never turns around. "We need to talk."

She shakes her head, her tropical scent filling my senses. "I have nothing to say."

"Even better, because I have plenty. So, I'll talk, you listen," I whisper. My breath dances over her skin as goosebumps rise on it.

"This is a bad idea Rathe. Someone might see us."

I chuckle. "Did it ever occur to you that maybe I don't care anymore?"

Sutton spins around so quickly that she slips through my grasp. I wasn't expecting her reaction so I wasn't at all prepared. "That's bullshit. You only care about racing. It's clear as day so don't come at me acting like two weeks with me suddenly made me more important because I'm not. I don't need you to pretend this was all something it wasn't. I'm a big girl and I can take care of myself so if you'll excuse me, I'd like to use the restroom and get back to the gala and help orphaned girls. I want to make a difference with this career. I want to help people. This is more than racing for me. I'm not like you."

"What the hell is that supposed to mean?" I ask. Her words sting more than she could possibly know. She has no idea that one of my biggest insecurities is being seen as just another racing playboy with no moral compass or respect for the world around me. Only Maxton and maybe Ryann know that.

Sutton looks away, guilt takes over her stance as she shrugs. "Exactly how it sounds."

"Wow," I say in a whisper. I'm shocked. "We spent the better half of two weeks getting to know one another and you still think so little of me?"

When she raises her head her eyes look smokey gray, like that smoke in the middle of a blazing fire. "Well, we might know each other's bodies but I still know next to nothing about you and you didn't even know that I grew up in the foster system so I mean when you think about it, how much do we really know?" Her question hangs between us. My insides churn because I feel like I'm trying to hang on for dear life but it feels like she's trying her hardest to pull away, to say goodbye before we ever got to say a proper hello. "We were meant to be rivals from the moment I got out of that car on the track. Let's just leave it be." She turns around and opens the bathroom door and disappears behind it. I stare at the door as if she'll suddenly reappear but she doesn't. With each passing second, I know that she's slipping away. I can't fight for her if she's not willing to try and fight for herself. If she would just listen to me…

As I stand there an idea forms in my head. It's the only way I know how to show her I care. Sadly, it'll take the race season before she knows what I've done to try and prove to her that these last two weeks weren't just about being lonely for me. All I can do is hope she'll hang on until then. If she does, she'll see I choose her.

Forty-Two

Sutton

Today is the day. I haven't been sure I was ready for it but it's too late now. The past week and a half, my team and I have spent every last minute making sure my car was race ready. The first race of the season kicks off tomorrow in Texas. My car is already there and I will fly out this afternoon...with Rathe. That's the part I'm not sure I'm ready for. We've seen a lot of each other after the press tour as we prepared our cars for the season. However, we haven't had time to talk, thankfully. I miss him more than I want to admit. While at the track I often find myself watching him as discreetly as possible. I don't know how or when I got so attached to him. It's not like me. I don't get attached to anyone because I know better. Attachment only leads to hurt because once you become attached, you're vulnerable and that means the person has the power to hurt you. I know I made the right decision when it comes to Rathe but it doesn't make me miss him less. When I saw him with that woman, I knew I could never compare to what he's become accustomed to in this world. I'm mediocre compared to the women he usually has on his arms. It was just a matter of time before he realized it too. So, I walked away before he could. I hurt myself before he could hurt me worse.

I sigh as I roll my suitcase to the front door. Evanna stands up from the couch. "You look sad, Sutton."

I shake my head and plaster on a smile for her. "I'm fine, really. You're just making a big deal out of nothing."

"I don't think I am and don't forget that I know you better than anyone. I know that fake smile when I see one. So, don't even try to pass that one off on me. I know that as much as you are looking forward to racing and that experience that you are also worried about being around Rathe," Evanna tells me.

I scoff and roll my eyes. "I am not." Sometimes, I forget just how well Evanna knows me.

Evanna laughs. "You are too. Have you talked to him?"

My nose scrunches up at the idea. "No, why would I?"

"Because you like him."

"No, I don't. We just had a fling and now it's over. It should have never happened in the first place but it did. Let's move on," I tell her.

"Okay, sure. So, the talk about risking your contract for love was just my wild imagination?" Evanna asks as she crosses her arms over her chest. Her look is serious and I know I'm not getting out of this house without some form of interrogation.

I shrug and look away. I busy myself with my luggage tag. "Momentary lapse of judgement."

"Bullshit and you know it Sutton. This is what you do and I love you but it drives me crazy."

Taking a deep breath I turn around to face her. "What exactly do I do?"

"You hide away from the world. You keep everyone at arm's length and act indifferent constantly. It's a really great act but it's still an act. It's unfair to you. I wish you could see that," Evanna tells me.

I want to instantly deny what she's saying even though I know it's true. "Look, I love you but I don't need a psychoanalysis right now. I need to get my head in the game because I have a race to win and Rathe is the last thing on my mind." The lie and sound of his name taste like acid on my tongue. I want to cringe but stand my ground as I step forward and pull her into a hug. "I'll see you when I get back."

"Okay, be safe and good luck. I can't wait to watch it," she tells me.

As I head outside the car is pulling up into our driveway. I meet the driver with my bag and climb inside. There was a moment before I climbed into the backseat that I was worried Rathe would be inside. Luckily, he's not. I sigh in relief but then that feeling of missing him hits me again. It's ridiculous I didn't even know him that well. I mean we had barely started to get to know one another. I really don't have a lot of reason to be so attached to Rathe but there was this feeling of comfort and safety with him. I keep thinking that though over and over but I miss that feeling.

The ride to the airport is a quiet one and we reach our destination. I only find Jowanna on the plane. "Hey, how are you?" I ask her.

She looks up from her phone. "Oh, I'm great. How are you?"

"I'm good. Is Rathe running late?" I ask, trying to sound normal.

Jowanna shakes her head. "No, he flew out last night. He had some kind of meeting early this morning so it's just us girls."

She smiles up at me and I do my best to return the smile. I have to act normal and normal me would be happy Rathe isn't going to be on the plane. "Awesome. Do you have any new earrings?" For the rest of the plane ride we talk about everything and I buy Evanna more earrings than necessary but I know she'll love them. Despite having something to keep my mind occupied, it still wanders off to Rathe multiple times. By the time we land in Texas I'm feeling antsy and not just about the race tomorrow.

****

I'm pretty sure I'm going purely on an hour of sleep and a gallon of coffee at this point. Last night, I went to bed early after grabbing some food so I could be ready for today. However, as soon as I laid down, I knew I'd never get any sleep. My nerves were beyond wired. My head starts to run through every possible outcome for today. When my wakeup call rang out through the silent room I felt as if I had just barely shut my eyes. Somehow, I got myself ready and made it to the elevator bay of the hotel, where I'm currently standing.

"You shouldn't stress about it so much." His voice skims over my skin, lighting everything on fire in its wake.

I give him a quick side glance and note just how good he looks. It should be a crime to just always look this good but give off the vibe of just not caring to the world. It's a dangerous combination and completely unfair. "Easy for you to say," I mumble quietly.

"You forget a couple of years ago I was exactly where you are right now. I know how scary it seems. It's unknown but I promise the minute the flag drops and you push the pedal down, it all changes. It's not scary, it's a rush. It won't feel any different from what you did on the streets because at the end of the day it's just racing. The road might look different, the car might look different but it's all just racing." Rathe never looks in my direction while he speaks, he just stares straight ahead at the elevator bay. The elevator pings and the doors slide open, Rathe steps forward inside of the space too small for the both of us. I don't follow. I'm frozen in place. He turns to face me and for the first time our eyes meet. The doors begin to shut and he throws his arm out to stop them. "Are you coming?'

My tongue is suddenly so dry I can't speak so I shake my head. "I forgot something in my room." A sadness comes into his eyes and I look away. He doesn't say another word and not soon enough the doors slide closed separating us once again. I sigh because now I feel even more off than I did earlier. I wait as the elevator moves up and down a few times before finally calling it back to my floor and riding down to meet Jowanna. Today is going to be a long day and it doesn't look promising that I'll have a happy turn out if the moment with Rathe was any indication.

Forty-Three

Rathe

My first thought when I wake up in the hotel room is...the second race of the season. I sigh and let the weight of today and this race weigh on my shoulders. I need to win this race. I completely messed up in the first race of the season. Between the stress of just being on the track and issues between Sutton and I, my anxiety hit an all time high in the middle of the race. Sutton had been the one to calm it so when I lost that connection to her, I lost the calm and I have lost her in every way possible.

As I sit up my mind goes back to the first race of the season which was only a couple of weeks ago yet it feels like a different lifetime altogether. That race opened my eyes. Sutton placed in third and I couldn't have been happier for her but there was a part of me that envied her. I was her until that damn wreck. I came in seventh which is not good. There's so much riding on this race season and there's no time to be coming in that low. However, I was doing great and holding a strong second position until halfway through the race when one of the other drivers blew a tire and spun out on the track. Luckily, it was a clean spin out but my anxiety went through the roof. Instantly, I backed off my speed and aggressive driving and soon enough I was in the back of the pack.

After the race I realized that I seriously needed help to manage my anxiety. Sutton had tried and succeeded as long as it was just the two of us on a track but that's not an option for this career. So, I started seeing a therapist and now I take some medication to help balance the anxiety. I definitely feel better, at least with that side of things.

I had a goal to get Sutton to talk to me after the race but when we finally got to leave the track, she had some unexpected visitors. Evanna and Jakob, Sutton's ex-boyfriend, had surprised her by showing up for the race. Ryann filled me in on everything because apparently, they had sat with her. The way Sutton had hugged and joked around with Jakob made that little green jealous monster rear its ugly head once more. I didn't know why Jakob was her ex-boyfriend but something told me he was a douche bag with a capital D. I didn't like the guy. He seemed too busy checking out every single female within a hundred yards and not nearly busy enough paying attention to Sutton. I didn't understand what he was thinking. Whenever Sutton was around, I couldn't seem to take my mind off her. Something told me that Jakob had been the one to mess up their relationship and that Sutton ended it because of that.

So, I adjusted my plan. I would just talk with her when we flew back home but then Jowanna had invited Ryann, Evanna and Jakob to fly back with us so that went up in flames pretty quickly. The third plan was to catch her at the track during practice but since I started seeing the therapist my track time has been different from hers and every time, I have seen her, Jakob has been around. The guy is really starting to get on my nerves. I'm hoping today I can actually talk to her.

After a shower and getting dressed I head down to the lobby to grab some breakfast before I meet up with my team and head to the racetrack. As I enter the restaurant located in the hotel, I spot Maxton and Ryann at a table. They're heads are leaning over the table and they seem to be whispering pretty angrily. I don't want any part of that so I head in the opposite direction but Ryann spots me anyways. "Rathe!" I turn around and see her waving me over. Reluctantly, I head their way. "What? Did you think you could sneak by that easily?"

"One can hope," I tell her as I sit down at the table.

Maxton nods. "Did you get any sleep last night?"

I nod. "Yeah, I did. How about you guys?"

"Fine," Ryann replies without looking up from her plate. Her attitude is weird today. She seems less like herself. "So, how are you feeling with the medication?"

"Better than I expected. I think that's why I've been getting more sleep than normal. It's very calming."

"That's great," she replies but she's definitely not her enthusiastic self.

The table falls silent. Eventually, I ask, "Are mom and dad coming in today?"

"Yeah, they're already here. They're just sleeping in. Oh, there's Sutton, Evanna and Jakob." Ryann stands up and calls them over, ignoring my groan. Before I know it we have a table full of people and everyone is listening to Evanna and Ryann talk fashion. I've tuned the two of them out and I'm currently focused on Jakob's hand as he plays with a lock of Sutton's hair. He catches me and smirks in my direction. I'd like to cross this table and knock that smirk clear off his damn face but something tells me that wouldn't help my case with Sutton.

I spot Colton and his crew chief, Becks, as they enter the restaurant. Thank goodness for saving graces because I actually need to talk to him. I stand up. "If you guys will excuse me, I have something I need to take care of before the race."

Ryann shoots up from her seat. "Oh, well darn." She pulls me into her arms. "Good luck and burn rubber."

I laugh. That has been our catch phrase since I first started driving a car. It always makes me smile when she repeats it.

"Thanks. See you in the pit," I tell Maxton before I turn around and head towards my next problem. At least this one I can solve.

****

This track is one I love. I let the sun warm my skin as I close my eyes and lean my head back. The sun beats down on me and I say a silent prayer for today. I need it. Too much is riding on this race season and I just keep adding more pressure to myself. Colton and I both know what needs to happen today but the question is can I pull it off? I have my worries of course and I know he does too but I feel better than I have in a long time. I walk over to Maxton. "How's the car?"

"Perfect or at least as close as it can be. How are you feeling?"

I nod. "As close as I can be to perfect myself."

"Did everything go okay with Colton this morning?"

I nod. Maxton is the only one who knows what's going on between Colton and I. I'd love to tell Ryann but she would never be able to keep it a secret. "Yeah, of course he has concerns and what happens today could very well end this entire plan but I can do this. I can place in the top three and prove that I'm worth putting money on."

"I know you are. I'd bet everything I have on you. You can do this. Just remember to breathe through the anxiety and don't let off that pedal." Maxton smiles at me and pats my back. His words of wisdom are exactly what I need right now.

I head to my trailer to grab a few Sour Patch Kids gummies for good luck. All too soon there's a knock on the door letting me know it's time. I pull my jumpsuit up and step out. Sutton is the first thing my eyes land on. She's about fifteen yards away, heading towards her car and she looks amazing. God, I miss her.

I allow myself a moment to watch her before I get my head in the game and zone everything going on around me out.

By the time I reach my car I'm clear headed and focused. My pit crew does the last minute run through while Maxton barks orders at them. He makes sure my suit and helmet are secure before knocking on the top of my helmet four times. Another one of those good luck rituals. Once I slide into the car everything becomes a blur. We move to our lineup and wait for the flag. "Deep breaths my brother, deep breaths," Maxton tells me just before the flag drops and the cars lunge forward in a race we'll never forget.

Forty-Four

Sutton

I wake up and feel the warmth next to me. My smile is instant until I remember it's not Rathe but Jakob beside me. Quietly, I crawl out of the bed. What the hell am I doing? I mean yes Jakob and I have history but that's not necessarily a good thing. Our past hasn't always been good and despite how sweet and encouraging he's been lately I still have my doubts. I still don't trust him. To be honest, Jakob has never given me much reason to trust him. I know a lot of why I'm spending time with him is to dull the ache of missing Rathe. I don't know how I allowed myself to grow so attached to him in such a little amount of time.

The sixth race of the season is tomorrow. I need to pack for it but right now I just need a break from life. In the dark I get dressed before I quietly leave the house and head for the one place, I've always been able to outrun my life. When I pull up, I almost turn back around and leave because I see Rathe's truck sitting in the lot. For a long time I sit in the parking lot staring at this truck. I know I need to suck it up. He's my teammate and I can't avoid him forever. It's not his fault I messed up and made what happened between us out to be more than it was. It's also not his fault I became a jealous mess when I saw him with that girl. Technically, I owe him an apology but that doesn't mean he'll get one from me.

Eventually, I decide that I just need to be an adult about all of this. Part of the issue is I don't know how to be an adult about all of this when it comes to Rathe. He made me feel so much so quickly. It was overwhelming and scary but then he reminded me that in this world I'm always second best. My head hasn't been on the track at all! My first official race went better than I could have hoped. I placed third which was amazing but it all went downhill from there. I've stayed in the fourth and fifth position for the last four races but it's not where I want to be. The only silver lining is that Rathe has been on the top three every race aside from the opening. It's been amazing to see him really drive again. Of course, Colton Donavan is leading the pack at the top of his game, as always.

I'm surprised when I hit the stands but see no car on the track. Instead, I see Rathe sitting on the front row, his head down, resting in his hands. I can tell by the hunch of his shoulders that something is bothering him. I'm not sure why I move towards him but my feet seem to follow my heart's desire and not my head's logic these days. He must hear me as I approach because he looks up as I reach him. "Sutton."

"Hey, I didn't expect to see you here." I'm not sure what to do so I just stand awkwardly halfway to him. A huge part of me wants to close the distance, climb into his lap and wrap my arms around his neck while kissing him as if my next breath depends on him. I won't do that but I want to so damn badly but he'll never know that.

Rathe nods his head slowly. "Yeah, I couldn't sleep tonight."

I let the silence hang between us for a minute to see if he is going to elaborate but when he doesn't, I know I need to say something. I mean, we might be on odd terms right now but I'm still here for him. "Do you want to talk about it?"

The heavy sigh that comes from his body breaks a part of my heart for him. "It's just I thought I was moving past this shit. I was really driving again for the first time since the wreck. I was winning and my anxiety was there but it wasn't controlling me like it had been. Then tonight I had a nightmare, a flashback is more like it and everything goes to shit again."

I step towards him as he stands and starts to pace back and forth along the fence that separates the stands from the track. His hands run through his hair relentlessly and every muscle in his body is tense. "Was the nightmare about the wreck?"

A laugh that sounds more strangled than any other sound I've ever heard comes from him. "It wasn't about the wreck...it was the wreck. Playing out in my mind in a very clear, very slow motion kind of way. You know the kind where it just messes with your head until you can't see straight?" I nod in response. "It was one of those!"

"Oh Rathe," I start to say but he cuts me off.

"No, don't give me that sympathy crap," he bites out.

I step back, completely caught off guard. "I wasn't."

"Yes, you were. You accused me of the same thing the night of the Corporate Cares gala. You didn't want it and you should understand that I don't want it either."

Technically he's right but I just want to help. "Rathe, that's a little harsh isn't it? I'm just trying to help."

"And I wasn't? I mean you think I was just playing some sick game with you. I wasn't but it didn't stop you from walking away from me and running right back to your ex, did it?" When he spins around to look at me I see so much emotion in his eyes that I have to look away. He closes the distance between us, wraps a hand around the back of my neck and pulls me into him until his mouth crushes down on mine. This kiss is everything and too much all at the same time. It steals the air from my lungs while giving my body the freedom to float. He pulls away, we're both breathless, his forehead rests against mine. "He's not right for you. You'll see it. By the end of the season you'll know I meant everything I didn't say but tried to show. I could have loved that fearless girl on the track full of spunk and sass. Bring her back to me. Don't run away from me Sutton."

His scent engulfs me and makes me feel safe even if I know it's just a ploy my mind is doing. I know that no one is ever truly safe. Rathe's words are beautiful but they'll be what breaks me if I let them. I take a moment to let them sink in because I still selfishly want them. Taking a deep breath, I breathe him and save it to my memory. "Rathe, I owe you an apology for trying to make this more than what it was. I got carried away but you can't love me because you don't know me. You and I would never work out. I mean the contract was enough reason for us not to happen without everything else. Now, there's Jakob that I have to consider in everything as well."

"You're kidding me, right?"

"No, we have a history and that means something but I'm still here if you need to talk," I offer.

Rathe shakes his head. "He's using you Sutton. I can see it and I don't even know the douchebag but you'll see. At the end of the season you'll know that somehow the two of us are meant for one another. You're mine Sutton, plain and simple. Run for now but eventually I'm going to catch up and you won't be able to lie to me or yourself when I do." Rathe wraps an arm around my abdomen and pulls me into him, pressing a kiss to my temple before he walks away.

My knees are weak and I have to sit before I fall. Tears slip from my eyes because I know Jakob isn't the one for me. I'm using him to hide behind but Rathe sees that and what does he mean by wait until the end of the season? I stare at the empty, dark track until my eyes dry and my head has more questions that it could possibly handle. When I stand up, I decide I have to focus on me and my racing. I have to forget about Jakob and I have to forget about Rathe...even if that seems impossible.

Forty-Five

Rathe

We're down to the last five races of the season. I've been staying high in the rankings which has been great for me and the sponsors. Colton Donavan has been winning basically everything but I'm good with that. We're both working towards the same goal right now. Sutton has managed to snag a couple of third places but mostly she's been staying just right outside the top three positions. Overall, though for her rookie years it's been great.

I watch her every damn chance I get but I haven't talked to her since the night she showed up at the track and I laid my claim on her. It seemed like the right thing to do at the time but now I don't know. She's still with Jakob and I guess somehow, I had been hoping that she'd come back to me after I made the confession. Instead, it's seemed to have pushed them closer together. Jakob still isn't trustworthy, I'm sure of that but I have no proof to make her believe me. So, I just have to wait for her to figure it out on her own or until the end of the season when she sees what I've been doing for her.

Dr. Panko, an older man with thinning gray hair and wire rim glasses that he wears low on his nose, studies me from his chair across the room. "So, you've been doing very well in racing, how does the anxiety feel?"

I nod my head as I think about it. "It feels a lot better than it did. I'm thankful for that. Like you said I still have my moments or days but it's much better than it was. It's manageable."

"That's so good. I'm glad to hear it," he says. "What about things with Sutton?"

My sigh is heavy because this is the subject that I don't want to talk about. I don't have an answer for him so I shrug. "I honestly don't know. I did as you suggested. I told her she was it for me but she's still with her ex-boyfriend. For now, that's all I can do."

"What about the plan Rathe? I mean you're doing it for her so I'm sure that would change her decision."

"It might and it might not. I don't know anymore. Sutton needs to come to her own decision. I'm hoping she'll do it before she finds out what I've been working on this season. I don't want to sway her decision based on my plan. I want her to want to be with me on her own." I explain. Dr. Panko is the one that made me truly realize just how much I've come to care for Sutton. I had let her into my world on a different level from any other girl I'd been with. Sutton was a siren's call that I had to answer.

The doctor nods his head. "I hear what you're saying Rathe but I still suggest you tell her."

I chuckle. "I think I'll pass on that suggestion for now. The last one didn't work out so well."

"But it did…"

My eyebrows pull together in confusion. "Well, Sutton and I are still avoiding each other so I'm not sure how that worked out."

"Rathe, from my point of view, it was less about getting the two of you together and more about you releasing the anxiety you had attached with the feelings you had developed for her. Once you voiced what you were feeling the anxiety over them lightened or disappeared. That was my goal." Dr. Panko looks over at me and with a smirk on his face.

I scoff. "Well, I'll be damned. I didn't see that one coming but you're not wrong now that I think about it."

222

"I know. It's my job and that's our time. You're doing great. Just keep up the good work," he says as he stands and leads me to the office door, with a pat on my back.

"See you next time," I tell him. As I leave out of his building, I pull my baseball cap down low and slip on my sunglasses. I'm trying to blend in with the rest of the people on the sidewalk because the last thing I need is the press to catch wind of my anxiety. They'd have a field day with that. It'd blow up quicker than the next sex scandal. I make a mental note to grab Ryann's birthday gift while I'm out in town today. As I'm walking down the sidewalk towards the little boutiques that she loves so much I pass a handful of little restaurants. Most have outside eating areas because the weather is often pretty enough to eat outside under canopy.

I pass the bistro that Maxton and Ryann have been raving about when I hear a familiar voice. "Ally, baby, come on. You know why I'm doing this."

"You promised it'd only be a week and it's been like two months now," the girl whines.

Jakob huffs. I quickly pass them and take a seat behind them, making sure to keep my head down. "Look, you know I need the damn money if not I'm going to start losing fingers so get off my case."

"She's your ex-girlfriend."

"Yeah, I'm aware. She's a bitch but she's also a means to an end. Once I get the money I'll be done and we can go back to just being the two of us," Jakob tells the girl.

My blood boils as I hear him talk about Sutton and using her. I knew he was a piece of shit but I had no idea it was this bad. I mean it's one thing to play games with her it's another to use her. I can't just stand around and let it happen. I order a glass of tea and wait for the right moment. I listen to Jakob make empty promises and say a lot of obscene things to the girl sitting across from him. It makes me sick to have to listen to him. Finally, he gets up to go to the restroom. After a few minutes I make my way to the back of the bistro where the restrooms are located. They are single restrooms so I'm waiting outside the door marked 'Mens'. Jakob opens the door and the smile on his face falls when he sees mine.

I grab him by his shirt and force him back inside the bathroom, slamming the door closed with my foot, without looking I reach around and lock it before continuing to the wall. Jakob's back slams against it. "You know I knew I didn't like or trust you. I knew you were a no good son of a bitch but I had no idea you would actually stoop so low. I thought I was just jealous because you had Sutton but it turns out I was right. You're using her."

His eyes widen before his mask falls back into place. "Look man, I don't know what you think you heard but you've clearly got your wires crossed. I'm not using anyone."

"Oh really? It's not just about getting money out of Sutton to keep your fingers?" I ask.

Jakob laughs. "As if anyone would believe you."

I cock my head to the side and smile. "Something tells me they would. Maybe, I should just tell Sutton about Ally."

"Ally's my cousin," Jakob spits out.

I laugh before I yank him back and slam his back against the wall again. "I just sat there and listened to the multiple dirty things you want to do with her. I even listened to her refer to it as sexy sex time so I highly doubt she's your cousin."

Silence hangs between us. "Sutton and I have history. You screwed up when you showed up with another chick on your arm. I have Sutton. I can always have Sutton, however and whenever I want. Our history tops whatever fling you had with her. She's a hot piece though, isn't she?"

My anger gets the best of me and before I even think about it I punch his jaw and let him slide to the floor. "Don't ever talk about her like that again." I begin to pace back and forth while his sick laughter fills the small bathroom.

"It's a shame really. You seem to actually care for her," he says as he wipes the blood from his lip. He gets to his feet and pushes past me.

I pinch the bridge of my nose as I hear the door unlock. The next words out of my mouth are the last thing I expected to say but they're the only way to save Sutton. "How much?"

Forty-Six

Sutton

As I enter the living room, I notice Evanna and Ryann sitting on the couch binge watching, To All The Boys I Loved Before. I secretly love this movie but it's not something I'll admit out loud even though I'm pretty sure Evanna knows. I take a seat in the chair, opposite of them and check my phone again. Jakob and I had plans but I haven't heard from him much over the last few days and even then, he was full of excuses and one word texts. Then yesterday he went completely silent but I got ready for the date regardless because knowing him, he'll show up like everything is fine. After almost an hour and still no sign of Jakob, Evanna pauses the movie. "I'm assuming you had plans with Jakob tonight."

"Why would you assume that?" I ask her.

She rolls her eyes. "One because I know you but even if I didn't let me list the ways. You're dressed up like you're ready to go out. You've checked that phone about every three to four minutes and you have your suspicious face on."

"I don't have a suspicious face."

Evanna and Ryann both laugh. "I barely know you and I know you have that face," Ryann says.

"It's just strange. He basically ghosted me when things seemed to be okay a few days ago," I explain.

Evanna shakes her head. "It's Jakob, what do you expect?"

"What do you mean?" I'm confused by her reaction. I thought she was on board with this whole Jakob situation after everything went down with Rathe. She seemed to be at least but now I'm not so sure.

"I love you but Jakob is nothing but a player. For some reason you don't see that in him but it's there. I don't like to use cliché sayings like once a cheater always a cheater but it's normally pretty true. Jakob has never done one thing for you. He's never given you a reason to even want to be with him. I say this with love but you're avoiding and you're using Jakob as a shield." Evanna gives me a pointed look.

I roll my eyes and play naive even though I know exactly what she's going to say. "I don't know what you're talking about."

"The hell you don't," Ryann chimes in. My eyes widen because I'm shocked by her outburst. "I'm sorry but you and my brother are crazy! You are both scared and running around trying to avoid one another and it's so dumb. You're both into each other so why not just be together?"

I scoff. "Maybe, because there's an entire clause in our contracts that basically forbids it."

"Oh please, what is Revv-It Racing going to do? Do you really think they would release both of their drivers from their contracts because they're having a relationship? Even if they did let one of you or both of you go from the contract another team would snatch you up in a heartbeat. Rathe has made a hell of a comeback this season and for a rookie season you've been insanely great. Regardless of the Revv-It contact you'd both be fine," Ryann explains. She gives me a small smile of encouragement.

Ryann's words roll around in my head and embed there. There's a really good chance she's right and if she is then I'm literally playing a game with both Rathe and Jakob because I know who I want to be with. It scares the hell out of me to let someone in but he's already there. He's been there, under my skin, since the first day on the track. It's Rathe. I check my phone but instead of looking for a text I'm checking the time. Rathe should still be at the track. I jump up from the chair and grab my keys as I head for the door. "If Jakob shows up just tell him I had an emergency and I'll catch up with him later." I'm out the door before Evanna or Ryann can reply.

Lucky for me, there's little to no traffic on the road and I find myself pulling into the track parking lot in record time. Sure enough, I spot Rathe's truck along with most of his pit crew's vehicles. Patrick's vehicle is parked beside a Honda Civic that looks an awful lot like Jakob's. I don't think much of it as I jog towards the entrance. Patrick waves me through with a big smile on his face. "You're not on the schedule today."

"No, I'm not but I need to see Rathe," I explain, slightly breathless.

Patrick's smile broadens. "Last I saw he was heading towards his room."

"Thank you!" My feet pick up to a faster speed as I get closer to the door that leads me down the hall to our rooms. However, as I approach the back half of the hallway that holds multiple doors, two of which belong to Rathe and I, voices echo in the quiet.

I slow to a walk to try and make out what is being said. I'm not usually nosey but something about these voices has the hair on the back of my neck standing up. Rathe's voice comes out, anger lacing every word. "You want more money? What the hell are you tied up in? What did you do with the ten thousand dollars I gave you two days ago."

"I owed some guys," the second voice replies. It stops me dead in my tracks because I know exactly who that voice belongs to. Jakob.

"You have a lot of audacity to show up here and demand more money from me. You have some kind of issue and you clearly need help or you wouldn't owe someone so much money. " Rathe's voice changes to suspicion.

Jakob sighs. "I like to gamble here and there. I just got in over my head."

"Well, I don't know what to tell you. I gave you ten thousand dollars. I'm not giving you another five. You'll have to figure it out. This was a one time thing," Rathe tells him.

It's silent for a bit and I'm so curious as to what the scene looks like right now. My mind is racing with the fact that Rathe gave Jakob ten thousand dollars to pay off a gambling debt. I mean why? What did he get out of it? It makes no sense to me.

"That's fine. I figured you'd say that. I'll just have to fix things between Sutton and I," Jakob tells Rathe.

My blood was pumping through my veins but now it's boiling. "You will leave her out of this. I gave you the ten grand you needed to keep her out of your mess. Don't cross me Jakob."

"Look, I need the money, one way or another. I can use you as my personal ATM or Sutton but at the end of the day, it's up to you who I use."

I step into their line of sight. Jakob's face washes with guilt and looks away. Rathe goes as pale as a ghost. "You've been using me this whole time?" I ask Jakob, who refuses to look at me. "And you knew and didn't bother to tell me?" I ask Rathe. His eyes lock with mine and I can see that he's begging me to understand but I can't. I can't understand any of this. Why would he not tell me about Jakob? "You know what, the two of you can have each other. I don't want to see either of you again," I tell them before I turn around and run back the way I just came.

I'm halfway down the tunnel, heading back towards the parking lot when I hear the footsteps behind me catching up. I try to run faster but I can't. I feel like I can't even breathe from all the emotions flooding me right now. When a hand closes around my elbow and yanks me around to face him, I shouldn't be shocked to find Rathe but I am. "Sutton, please let me explain."

"Now? Now you want to explain? You've had plenty of time to explain to me that my so-called boyfriend was actually only using me to pay off his gambling debt. There has been plenty of time for that," I yell at him, unable to control my voice.

Rathe runs his hands through his hair. "I didn't want you to find out. I didn't want you to get hurt. I only found out by accident. It was the other day when I was leaving a therapy session. I spotted Jakob and some girl, he called her Ally, sitting at a bistro on one of the outside seats. I took a seat behind him and listened in. I heard all about it so when he got up to go to the restroom, I followed him and told him to leave you out of it. He wasn't going to so I gave him the money," Rathe tells me. Everything comes out in a quick, hurried breath.

I shake my head as my anger wins. "You should have told me. I deserved to know. You know what the worst part is. I was coming here to tell you I wanted to give us an actual chance but then I find out you're just as bad as the rest of them. You've lied to me and kept secrets from me too so what's the point?"

"I'm not like Jakob," he bites out.

"You don't even see it but you are. You lied to me just like he did."

Rathe blows out a breath. "I shouldn't have lied and I'm sorry for that, I really am but there is a difference. I lied to protect you. He lied to use you and if you can't see that difference then I don't know how to help you." We stare each other down until my anger starts to ease and the hurt begins to work it's way through my body. Defeat and betrayal are two things I don't like to feel but right now they are both weighing on my shoulders. "You're just looking for a reason to run. You may have come here with the intention of giving us a chance but really, you're looking for a reason to run and you found one. This is what you wanted." Rathe holds his arms out to the side of him in a challenge. One that I hear loud and clear.

I shake my head no, dismissing his words. "No, this is just the tip of the iceberg of what I wanted and why I came here tonight."

"What?" His bewildered look should make me laugh but it can't, not at this moment. Everything is so heavy.

"I wanted the whole damn iceberg, not just the tip. I wanted to crash into it like the Titanic and drown in the icy cold water it sits in. I wanted to be consumed by it...by you. I wanted you. I wanted the guy from the press tour that made my skin spark with fire and challenged me in ways I never knew possible but it's obvious I was wrong. You're not him," I tell him as I look away. The sigh that leaves my body is heavy and I turn around and walk away from Rathe, my heart crumbling. It's sad how much harder it is to walk away from him than Jakob even though I have history with Jakob. Rathe doesn't follow me and I'm conflicted by that. Part of me wanted him to fight for me but the other part just wants him to let go because once again I'm reminded, I'm not worth the fight.

Forty-Seven

Sutton

I'm standing in my mirror once more. I never thought I'd see the day where I spend so much time getting dressed and doing my hair and makeup. It also never crossed my mind that I'd actually own a few fancy gowns. They had never seemed like a necessary part of my life until recently. There's a lot of things that didn't seem necessary until recently. I sigh as the past few months of my life replay through my mind like a movie reel. The race season is officially over. Colton won the cup but Rathe managed to pull in second and I came in fifth, which is good for a rookie. It was amazing to be a part of but it was bittersweet. A large part of me wanted to run to Rathe and congratulate him but I knew I couldn't. Our personal issues kept me from reacting any other way than professional.

My personal life is the real issue though that weighs so heavily on me. After finding out Jakob was using me, I cut all ties from him. I changed my number and blocked him from all social media. It's what I should have done when I caught him cheating the first time but I guess it's better late than never. Rathe though is another issue altogether. I can't cut ties from him. I can't avoid him even though I try my hardest. I don't know why but finding out that he had lied to me hurt worse than anything Jakob had done to me. Maybe, it's because I stopped expecting anything from Jakob a long time ago but there was still hope with Rathe.

A few days after I had caught Jakob and Rathe together, talking about the money, Rathe showed up at my house. I refused to answer the door so Evanna did. I had hid in the corner of the living room where I couldn't be seen but could still hear everything he had to say. The memory comes flooding back.

"Evanna, I know she's here and I know she's upset. She has every right to be. I messed up but I honestly was trying to protect her. My intentions were never to hurt her. I would never want that." I could hear the plea in his voice and it pulled at every fiber of my being.

Evanna believed him. I could tell by the look on her face. "I know but you know how hard it is for Sutton to trust someone. You kind of broke it after she gave it to you."

Rathe sighs. "I know. My intentions were in the right place but it was still wrong. I'm trying to fix it but she won't talk to me. She's changed her number so I can't call or text because believe me I tried until I found out it was disconnected. I don't want to approach her at the track because that's her job and I know how much it means to her. When I show up here she's never home. How am I supposed to ask for forgiveness if she won't let me see her?"

"You keep trying. Look, I don't blame you for how you handled things. Truth be told I probably would have done the same thing. Now, you just have to keep proving that you care. It goes further than you'd think," Evanna tells him.

I want to know what Rathe's face looks like right now because I know mine is shocked. To hear Evanna admit that she would have lied to me is shocking. I never would have guessed that. Now, I'm not sure how to feel about the way Rathe handled the situation. My stomach churns with unease. What if I'm overreacting? What if I'm running because it's less scary than staying and seeing where Rathe and I end up?

"Okay, well, may I give you this?" I see Rathe's hand extend a black envelope to Evanna. She takes it but the look of confusion on her face is priceless. "It's an event for Corporate Cares. I think Sutton should be there, you as well. I'm sure Rylee will be reaching out to invite her

personally but I wanted to be the first. It's the week after the final race of the season. Please, try and get her to come."

Evanna nods her head. "I will."

The knock on my bedroom door has the memory slipping from my mind. I turn to see Evanna looking like a princess in her red evening gown. She smiles at me when she sees me. "I swear every time I see you all dressed up like this, I'm breathless. You're gorgeous and don't even realize it."

"Okay, just stop right now before you make things weird or start crying." I walk away to the other side of the room.

She laughs. "Okay but you do look amazing. Purple was definitely the best decision."

As I turn back around, I catch a glimpse of myself in the mirror and I know she's right. The off the shoulder, beaded bodice, fit and flare plum gown is perfect. I feel more confident than I have in days. Although I'm not looking forward to tonight, I at least feel like I look the part. It's been a week since the race season ended. It's been a week of not seeing Rathe...I wish I could say it had made me feel better, but honestly it hasn't. I still miss him terribly and the confusion I feel over my feelings for him hasn't lessened. Tonight will be the first night I've seen him since the final race. I wouldn't even go if it wasn't for the fact that Rylee called and invited me a couple of days after Rathe gave the envelope to Evanna.

"Hey, are you okay?" Evanna asks.

I nod my head. "Yeah, I was just mentally preparing for tonight."

"I'm pretty sure that's not possible." Evanna gives me a small, tight smile. She's right. There's no way to prepare for this but I have to try. The doorbell rings and we exchange a look. "Did you order a car?"

I shake my head. "No, I thought we agreed to drive ourselves."

"We did. I'll grab the door. You finish getting ready because we need to leave in a few," she tells me as she turns away and heads towards our living room.

I grab my clutch and head through our house. I'm shocked when I see Rathe standing on the doorstep, looking better than I even remember. His black and charcoal gray suit has my heart rate speeding up. "What?"

"I figured you ladies could use a ride." I open my mouth to protest but Rathe holds up his hand to stop me. "Before you start to protest Evanna already agreed to it so just go with it." My mouth closes and I scan the room for Evanna. I hadn't even realized she was missing until now. That happens when Rathe is around, the rest of the world just falls away. "She's already in the car. I'm just waiting on you." I nod and cross the room and step out of the door. As I turn to shut the front door behind me, Rathe turns as well reaching for the door handle. His lips are a breath away and I have to fight every urge in me to pull him to me and claim his mouth like he's done to mine so many times before. I can smell his cologne and aftershave as it clings to his skin. "You look stunning," he whispers between us.

I allow myself to bask in his compliment for a moment before I yank the door shut and move away from him and towards the limo. I hear his footsteps behind me. When I reach the car, he's already on my heels, reaching around and pulling the door open. I slide in beside Evanna who avoids my eye contact. The limo ride is quiet and tense but at least we aren't delayed by traffic.

As soon as we make it inside Rathe disappears. I hate to admit it but I've been scanning the room for him ever since. I've mingled with just about everyone possible. I'm exhausted by the time we are seated and served drinks while the speeches begin. Rylee comes to the podium and I notice Colton and Rathe along with a couple of other guys standing behind her, off to the side. My curiosity rises.

"Thank you all for being here tonight. I know it's uncommon for us to have multiple events like this in the same year but this year has been outstanding for Corporate Cares. As most of you know we started a program for orphaned boys years ago and it has been growing bit by bit. This year someone very special asked, what about orphaned girls? Her question was one we had once asked ourselves but had been pushed to the back burner due to lack of funding. However, that changed this year. Thanks to Rathe McCall. He heard her question and made it a priority to see we got the funding we needed. Rathe McCall and my husband, Colton Donavan, spent every last second pulling in extra sponsors to help raise money for this very cause. For every race they placed the top three in, thousands of dollars was donated to Corporate Cares to fund the orphaned girls project. I'm so happy to be able to stand here tonight and tell you that we can finally make this plan a reality. Tonight we get to celebrate the new ways we will get to help children who need it. Now, Rathe McCall would like to say a few words." Rylee steps away from the podium. As she passes Rathe she gives him a quick hug, her smile large. If I thought my heart was racing on the porch about an hour ago...that was nothing. My heart has to be missing from my chest altogether now. I can't believe what I'm hearing.

Rathe gives the crowd his panty dropper smile. "Good evening everyone. Thank you for joining us. So, I hate to admit this but up until a few months ago I really didn't pay attention to what Corporate Cares was doing. I didn't think about orphaned children or their living situations. Then I met someone this year. Someone who knew all too well about the obstacles that children in the system face. She knew because she had been one herself. After discovering this I made it my mission this race season to help raise enough money to get this project up and running. I'm so happy that I could help. I'm so happy that I could learn and see how this amazing woman's life had been before I met her. I'm sure the things I've learned about how the system works doesn't come close to what she's experienced but it's a start. This woman has become a force to be reckoned with. She came into my life and saved me from the pits of hell that consumed my soul. She taught me how to find myself in the fire. I admire her determination, sass, strength and courage. The fact that she never gives up and yet is always there for others. Somewhere along the way I didn't just fall for her. I fell in love with her. Right now, she's probably dismissing that idea but once she has time to think about it, she'll know it's true." Rathe's eyes find mine in the crowd and his chocolate brown pools lock onto mine. "I did this for and because of you. Thank you for making me a better person without even realizing you were doing it. Please, forgive me for the mistakes I made and give us a real chance, the way that Colton, the handful of sponsors, Corporate Cares and myself were able to give to some orphaned girls, stuck in the system feeling as if they don't belong anywhere."

Rathe steps away from the podium and I rise to my feet. I'm not thinking I'm just moving. Evanna had taken my hand at some point during his speech. I watch as it falls to her side. Tears sting my eyes as I turn and make my way out of the room. I reach the lobby and the room begins to spin. I gasp for air but my chest feels so tight and heavy. "Sutton." I hear my name but it's so muffled. I feel his hands on my shoulders and once he's standing in front of me, I can make out his face through my blurry vision. "Shit, I think you're having a panic attack." He guides me to a nearby chair. "I'll be right back." He disappears and returns a few minutes later with water. I take a small sip. My world slowly comes back into focus. "Are you doing okay?"

I nod my head. "What was that in there?"

Rathe shrugs and looks away. "It's what I've been working on all season to try and get you to see how I feel."

"Why didn't you tell me?" I ask.

He laughs. "When was I supposed to tell you Sutton? Neither of us have the best communication skills."

I sigh. "Did you mean it?"

Rathe gets down to my level, gently he takes my face between his hands and I feel like I'm coming home once again. Why does it always feel like that with him? "Every single word. You turned my world upside down the day you came racing into it. I was certain you were meant to be my rival but I think it's so much more than that. You're meant to be the love of my life. I see that now. I know I hurt you. I know you're scared but I promise to protect you at all costs. You belong with me. You're mine Sutton."

Tears slip from my eyes as my heart stitches itself together. I've never belonged with anyone. I was always just passed from one person to another. When I met Evanna we had kindred spirits and we were able to rely on each other but somehow, she was still able to see the beauty in the world. I had lost that ability until Rathe was thrown into my life and gave me hope and made me see color in my black and white world. I think all this time I was looking for a place to call home. I never considered that it might be a person. A single person who finds your broken and fixes it without knowing. Rathe and I haven't had that much time together but somehow, he's pieced me together in ways I didn't know were possible. He scares the hell out of me but I want him in every possible way. I lean forward and lightly place my lips to his. My heart calms some more because it knows it's exactly where it's meant to be...finally. "I'm yours Rathe." Those three words are the hardest ones I've ever said but also the most honest. He smiles before leaning in to claim my mouth once more.

Epilogue

Rathe
6 months later

I stand at the kitchen counter waiting for the coffee to brew with the newspaper in my hand. The picture on the front page is an image I want to memorize into my mind forever. I can't take my eyes off her smile. As I lay the newspaper down, I look out into the backyard through the glass doors at the back of my house. The sunlight dances off the pool. Yesterday the first house for orphaned girls officially opened. Six girls have been placed in a stable environment where they get to have a family aspect with the counselors and workers from Corporate Cares. They don't have to worry about being moved around from one foster home to the next. The picture on the front page of that paper captures some of the girls along with Rylee and Sutton. Sutton looks so happy that it makes me feel on top of the world that I was able to help make that possible.

Over the past six months Sutton and I have grown so much both as individuals as well as a couple. We still have our days where she slips into her head and finds it hard to trust me even though she has no reason not to. It's her past that makes her feel that way and I understand. We make it through those days together. In the off season from racing we worked a lot with Corporate Cares and other various charity programs to help the community. I have to say this is the best I've felt in years.

Somehow, both Sutton and I, were able to keep our positions on Revv-It Racing. I had been prepared to step down and move to another team or retire, if necessary. I just knew that I couldn't not have Sutton in my life anymore. Luckily, it didn't come down to that. As long as we can keep our personal life off the track, they will allow us to be a couple. I tried to act like I wasn't shocked but I really was.

I don't know where we'll be in a year from now but I do know that as long as I have Sutton by my side, I'll be happy. She calms the storm of anxiety in my soul and I hope I bring her light to the darkness in hers. We've been a lot of things to one another since meeting but I know one thing for sure...she'll always be my rival when we meet on the track and the love of my life everywhere.

Authors Note

Want to keep up with all of the other books in K. Bromberg's Driven World? You can visit us anytime at www.kbworlds.com and the best way to stay up to date on all of our latest releases and sales, is to sign up for our official KB Worlds newsletter HERE.

Are you interested in reading the bestselling books that inspired the Driven World? You can find them HERE.

Extras

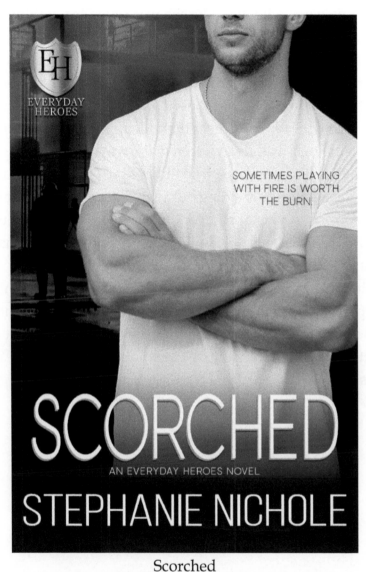

Scorched
K. Bromberg's Every Day Heroes World
Coming 2021

A poetic firefighter who is determined to make a difference in the world.

A broken girl who feels like she was saved for nothing.

Sometimes playing with fire is worth the burn.

Decker Holmes has known since he was a child he wanted to be a firefighter. He runs into burning buildings without a second thought or moment of hesitation. On his first call he saves a young girl with jade green eyes that still appear to him in dreams.

Arrietty Jones has always been in the way. She was constantly reminded of that growing up with her abusive, alcoholic father. One night changes everything but years later she's questioning if she was worth saving at all. Her life is a mess, and it isn't until a firefighter who seems so familiar comes into her life that she begins to think that just maybe, she's worth it after all.

With an arsonist on the loose, setting fires to everything in their path, the last thing Decker and Arrietty need is her ex-boyfriend reappearing to cause more trouble. Can Decker and Arrietty make their way out of the smoke or be engulfed in the flames?

Acknowledgements

First of all, thank you so much to K. Bromberg for allowing me to be a part of her worlds. It was a dream come true to be a part of this project. I loved revisiting one of my favorite series by one of my favorite authors and growing this world. Brining Colton and Rylee back to life was such an experience.

To my publishing company, Kingston Publishing, thank you for allowing me to take part of this world. Thank you for your continued support and faith in my stories and characters.

To my family, thank you so much for believing in me when I can't. You have instilled a love for books within in my soul and this is al possible because of you.

To my all-stars, my mom, Mary, Pat, Erika, Chasity and Julie, you girls are rock stars! I don't know how I would manage to finish a book without you. Thank you for sticking on this wild ride of Rivals with me. Through all the changes you never gave up.

To my guardian angels, auntie and VannaLynn, I truly believe that the two of you helped make this opportunity possible. Keeping rocking out heaven for the rest of us.

Last but certainly not least, thank you to the readers. If you've been with me for a while I can't thank you enough for all the support you have given me. When I want to give up, it's you guys that make me continue. If you're new to me thank you for taking a chance on Rathe and Sutton. I hope you love them.

About the Author

Stephanie Nichole lives in a small town with her family in New Mexico. She graduated college in 2010 with a degree in business and accounting. However, her true passion is all things book related. As a student English and Literature were her favorite subjects. Weekly library trips with her mother also helped instill her love for books. Stephanie would look forward to summer most of all, not because she was out of school but for the summer reading groups at her local library. After a friend's encouragement she started her author journey in 2016.

Stephanie writes in multiple genres but her main focus jumps between new adult romance and young adult fantasy romance. From time to time you will find her work to get a little dark but there is always a light at the end of the tunnel.

Stephanie recently announced that she will be a participating author in the K. Bromberg Worlds as well as Corinne Michaels Savlation Society and Vi Keeland and Penelope Ward's Cocky Hero Club. Keep a look out for her titles Rivals(Driven World), Scorched (Everyday Herores World), Stronghold (Savlation Society)and Supercilious Stud (Cocky Hero Club).

Stephanie is an avid book, music and old Hollywood movie lover. When she's not busy reading or writing she's probably binge-watching Netflix or PassionFlix. Some of her favorite authors are: Edgar Allan Poe, K. Bromberg, Abbi Glines, Colleen Hoover, Anna Todd, M. Robinson, Ilsa Madden-Mills, Teagan Hunter, Nicholas Sparks, Tarryn Fisher, Emily Bronte, Jane Austen, F. Scott Fitzgerald and Charles Dickens.

Stephanie also loves to connect with her readers on social media.

Reader's group: https://bit.ly/StephanieNicholeRG
Newletter: https://bit.ly/StephanieNicholeNL
Author page: https://bit.ly/StephanieNicholeFB
Bookbub: https://bit.ly/StephanieNicholeBB
Amazon: https://amzn.to/2WF23P0
Instagram: https://bit.ly/StephanieNicholeIG
Twitter: https://bit.ly/3dToJ4l
Goodreads: https://bit.ly/StephanieNicholeGR

Also Written by Stephanie Nichole

The James Brothers Series:
Pedal to the Metal
Breaking the Limits
Force of Impact
Need for Speed
Finish Line

The Furiously Fast Series:
Full Throttled
Dangerous Curves (Coming Soon)

The Dark Prophecy Series:
Magicals
Captured
Ignite

Bloody Mary's Curse:
Becoming Bloody Mary
Breaking Bloody Mary

K. Bromberg's Every Day Heroes:
Scorched (Coming March 2021)

Corrine Michaels' Salvation Society:
Stronghold (Coming Soon)

Vi Keeland & Penelope Ward's Cocky Hero Club:
Supercilious Stud (Coming Soon)

Other Titles:

Also Written by K. Bromberg